Kaylee's Grand-Slam

Joey Dolton

Published by Boro Publishing, LLC, 2024.

This is a work of fiction. Similarities to real people, places, or events are entirely coincidental.

KAYLEE'S GRAND-SLAM

First edition. May 31, 2024.

Copyright © 2024 Joey Dolton.

ISBN: 979-8989859276

Written by Joey Dolton.

Table of Contents

Chapter 1
The Red Hawks

L ittle Kaylee Dyer dashed through the dusty streets of her suburban neighborhood, her backpack bouncing against her narrow shoulders as she made a beeline for the local baseball field. It was a crisp autumn afternoon, the air tinged with the promise of change, but for Kaylee, there was only one thing on her mind: baseball.

As she rounded the corner, the familiar sounds of laughter and shouting greeted her ears, signaling that practice was already underway. With a burst of energy, Kaylee sprinted towards the field, her heart pounding with anticipation. She had been waiting for this moment all day, the chance to watch the boys play and maybe even sneak in a few swings of her own.

The high school baseball team, or any baseball team in the country really, had no females in their list of players, or room for any. It was commonly felt that women could not and should not play the sport. The game was of course dominated by the larger six-foot men who most people would have felt should be playing football instead. This saddened Kaylee a lot but never changed her love for the sport, even as a little girl, it was all she ever thought off.

As she reached the edge of the field, Kaylee skidded to a halt, her eyes widening with excitement as she took in the scene before her. The boys, clad in their mismatched uniforms, were scattered across the diamond, their coaches barking orders and offering words of encouragement. It was a sight that never failed to fill Kaylee with awe, the sheer power and athleticism of the players leaving her breathless.

For a moment, Kaylee stood on the sidelines, content to simply watch and soak in the atmosphere. But as she gazed longingly at the boys on the field, a familiar itch began to stir within her, a restless energy that demanded to be unleashed. Kaylee wanted nothing more but to at that fleeting moment to step into the field and demand a spot amongst the boys. The tall high school boys who could squash her and not even know.

Without a second thought, Kaylee darted onto the field, her eyes fixed on the nearest coach.

"Can I play too?" she called out, her voice tinged with excitement.

The coach, a burly man with a grizzled beard, glanced down at Kaylee with a bemused expression. He wanted to laugh, it was obvious, thinking that this was a joke and that she was only trying to show her excitement to watch. The coach gazed at her, his smile fading off, he realized at that moment that the young lady meant business.

"Sorry sweetheart," he said with a sympathetic smile. "This is boys' practice. Maybe you can find some other girls to play with.

As Kaylee's plea to join the practice was met with rejection, her determination only intensified. Ignoring the coach's dismissal, she glanced around quickly, waiting for the opportune moment to make her move. When the attention of the adults was momentarily diverted, she seized the chance and darted towards the equipment shed.

KAYLEE'S GRAND-SLAM

In the shadows of the shed, Kaylee's hand closed around the cool metal of a bat, her heart racing with anticipation. With a steely resolve, she emerged back onto the field, her eyes locked on the boy clutching a baseball.

"Throw it to me!" Kaylee called out, her voice ringing out unwavering determination. But instead of compliance, her demand was met with a chorus of protests from the coaches, their shouts echoing across the field.

"Get off the field girl!" one of the coaches bellowed, his face contorted with frustration. But Kaylee stood her ground, her grip on the bat tightening as she stared defiantly at the boy with the ball.

"Throw it to me!" Kaylee yelled even louder this time.

"Don't you dare throw that ball!" the coach yelled back at the boy. "Young lady, whatever your name is, get off the field now. You don't wanna hurt yourself, put that down."

"You've been doing this for years, have you ever hurt yourself? Why do you think I'll hurt myself?"

"Because you're a kid."

"So what are they then?" Kaylee responds, gesturing to the high school kids standing around, only enjoying the unfolding scene.

The coach remains silent, her words hitting him deep.

Kaylee grips the metal bat even harder, before turning her attention back to the kid with the ball and gives him this time a more stern glare. "Throw it!"

The kid stares back, seeing the building rage and determination in her eyes. He is tempted to throw but doesn't want to go against his coach's orders. However he fixes his stance, ready to throw at any moment.

With each passing moment, the tension on the field grew thicker, the air crackling with anticipation. Kaylee's heart pounded in her chest as she waited for the boy to make his move, her eyes never leaving the ball cradled in his hand. The rest of the coaches and the boys watched in anticipation, wanting the first coach's orders to be obeyed but desperately wanting to see if she would make the hit.

The coach wasn't having it anymore, he began to walk towards her to take the bat which ever way he could. Kaylee stared at the kid again, this time without words but demanding with her eyes, showing that she desperately needed him to throw that ball at her.

Suddenly, without warning, the boy's lips curved into a mischievous smile as he adjusted his stance. With a swift motion, he wound up and unleashed a powerful throw in Kaylee's direction.

Instinct took over as Kaylee swung the bat with all her might. Everything seemed to be in slow motion as her muscles strained against the force of her movement. WHAM!-The ball hit the net behind her. The coach stopped in his tracks, believing that his message has been passed already. Despite her best efforts, the ball sailed past her, leaving her feeling a mix of frustration and exhilaration. She put down the bat herself.

Before the coaches could intervene, Kaylee's eyes met the gaze of one of them, and whose expression held a glimmer of something unexpected. It was a look that spoke volumes, a silent acknowledgment of the fire that burned within her. He could see it, potential, and he felt it would be great one day, it would do big things and she felt it too.

As the coaches approached to usher her off the field, Kaylee felt a surge of defiance coursing through her veins. She refused to be fettered by their limitations or bound by their expectation. With a sense of purpose, she turned away from the field, her resolve unshakable.

Undeterred by the disapproving glares and harsh words that followed her, Kaylee made her way to the outskirts of the field. There, beneath the fading light of the setting sun, she took her place among the scattered stones and debris.

With a flick of her wrist, Kaylee sent a stone soaring into the air, her eyes tracking its trajectory with unwavering focus. As it arced gracefully through the sky, she swung a metal rod behind her back and swung it back in smooth motion, cutting through the wind, she smashed the rock with a hard hit that sent it swinging high into the air again, far away from her position.

In that moment, as she stood alone on the edge of the field, Kaylee Dyer knew that she was destined for greatness. With each stone that she sent hurtling into the air, she reaffirmed her commitment to chasing her dreams, no matter what!

———◉———

KAYLEE STOOD OUTSIDE her modest one-bedroom apartment in the tranquil enclave of Tien, a peaceful oasis nestled within the bustling city of Boston. Unlike the crowded streets and towering skyscrapers that characterized much of the city, this part of town was a haven of serenity and solitude.

Here, the houses were scattered sparsely along tree-lined streets, their quaint charm standing in stark contrast to the concrete jungle that lay beyond. It was a neighborhood reserved for those who preferred the quiet comforts of a suburban life over the hustle and bustle of the city living.

Kaylee retrieved the stack of mail from the mailbox, she flipped through ads, bill letters and one particular letter from a familiar sender, she immediately squeezed it and threw it away with a frown. She then looked around to make sure no one saw her, lucky her. She then breathed and took a moment to appreciate the tranquility that surrounded her. The air was crisp and clean, free from the cacophony of noise that often plagued the city streets. It was a place where time seemed to move a little slower, allowing its residents to savor the simple pleasures of everyday life.

With a contented sigh, Kaylee glanced down the long-stretched street that led to the heart of the neighborhood. There, nestled among the trees, lay a cluster of stores, malls, and restaurants, the essentials of modern living, albeit in a more subdued setting. It was a reminder that even in the midst of tranquility, the conveniences of city life were never far away.

Kaylee had blossomed into a vibrant and confident twenty-five-year-old woman, her brunette locks cascading in luscious waves down her back, framing her flawless complexion. With her curvaceous figure and magnetic charm, she was the epitome of a dream girl, turning heads wherever she went.

Even the usually composed mailman found himself momentarily entranced by Kaylee's beauty, forgetting his duty as he stood mesmerized on her doorstep. It wasn't until a sharp "WACK" to the back of his head from an irate old lady wielding a newspaper snapped him back to reality with a start.

Blinking away his daze, the mailman quickly regained his composure, shooting a sheepish grin in Kaylee's direction as she waved casually at him. With practiced ease, she shifted through the stack of mail in her hands, her perfectly manicured fingers gliding over bills, advertisements, and coupons with disinterest.

But then, nestled among the mundane clutter, Kaylee's eyes lit up with excitement as she spotted it, the envelope she had been eagerly anticipating. With a wide smile spreading across her face, she tore open the envelope with eager anticipation, her heart racing with excitement at what lay inside.

This smile better not change!

She tore open the envelope and pulled out the letter from the Boston Red Hawks Team Manager.

SHE MADE IT!

Kaylee Dyer stood on the threshold of her dreams, her heart pounding with a mixture of excitement and disbelief. She had done it, she had made history as the first female Major League Baseball player, a feat that had seemed impossible to many, but for her had been the culmination of years of dedication and perseverance.

From the moment she could walk, Kaylee had been enamored with baseball, much to the bewilderment of her parents and the amusement of those around her. While other girls her age were playing with dolls or dress-up, Kaylee was out in the backyard, swinging a makeshift bat and pretending to hit home runs in the World Series.

It all began when she was just a wide-eyed five-year-old, her grandfather taking her to to her first Boston Red Hawks game. From the moment she stepped foot in the stadium, Kaylee was hooked. The crack of the bat, the roar of the crowd, it was a sensory overload that left her breathless and eager for more.

As she grew older, Kaylee's obsession with baseball only intensified, much to the chagrin of her parents. They tried to dissuade her, pointing out that women didn't play baseball in the major leagues, but Kaylee refused to be swayed. With a stubbornness that bordered on obsession, she wore them down, her determination unyielding.

Her parents even attempted to redirect her passion towards softball, but Kaylee wouldn't hear of it. She had her sights set on the big leagues, and nothing, not even the prospect of playing a 'softer' version of the game could deter her.

So, it was with unbridled enthusiasm that Kaylee's mother signed her up for the local T-ball league. From the moment she stepped onto the field, it was clear that Kaylee was a force to be reckoned with. The coach, a grizzled veteran of the game, had no idea what he was in for when he welcomed her onto the team, thinking she'd be an extra hand that wouldn't really outshine anyone... not even the mascot.

Every practice, every game, Kaylee gave it her all, her passion for the sport evident, in every swing of the bat and every sprint around the bases. She was always the first to arrive, and was the last one to leave the field, often staying behind to help the maintenance crews rake and tidy up, it was like she couldn't just take in the idea of leaving the pitch. It wasn't long before she had become a fixture at the ballpark, her infectious energy lighting up the field and bringing a smile to the faces of all who knew her.

Despite the challenges and setbacks she faced along the way, Kaylee never lost sight of her ultimate goal; to play baseball at the highest level and prove to the world that anything was possible with hard work and determination, or whatever it is Oprah Winfrey had said.

The fact that she was a girl, and not to mention a young girl, did not stop her from being one of the best players on her team. This did not stop her doubters, but by God was she going to prove herself, and prove herself she did. Yes, it was a team effort, that she could not deny, though that she scored the most runs wasn't a fluke either. That and the fact that her team won every game that year, and she quickly moved onto the little league team, where she crushed it just as much.

As a baseball player, it was hard for her to deny the development of an ego. A lot of times, this would hurt her, to a tremendous degree. Other times, it would help her achieve her dreams, no matter the obstacles in the way.

In high school, the administration tried to stop her from playing baseball, saying she could only play softball. Despite these two sports being similar, Kaylee was outraged, and by this point, got her parents fully on her side. As a result they sued the school and the school district, and won.

In her senior year, the school was forced to make a coed baseball team, and they won the state championship, with Kaylee winning MVP.

After graduating high school, the first thing Kaylee did was enroll at a nearby university, with the purpose of pursuing her degree in Sports management. After a career as a player, the next obvious step would be to manage a baseball team, so it was a no brainier. In addition, she joined her universities baseball team as well, with them not even spearing to challenge her.

Then it happened. A scout for the Boston Red Hawks was there, watching the game. She actually had been approached by a scout for the Los Angeles Riders while in high school, but her parents had put their foot down and said she had to go to college. As a minor then, she had little choice. In the end, it was a good choice, considering it was the Red Hawks that started her obsession with the sport.

Against all rational thought, she decided not to play special that day. She was going to succeed on her normal merits, not ones that would burn her out. This gamble would pay off significantly, especially when the scout came along to see her after the game.

"Ms. Dyer?" The scout had called out, trying to catch her before she returned to the locker room after the winning game.

"Present", Kaylee replied, her tiredness evident in her voice. She had recognized him already, Harold Smith. She had studied everything and everyone about and in the Red Hawks, her dream team which was the hallmark team of Boston, her home town.

"Nice game today, really good work out there."

"I'm sorry, you are?"

"Oh how rude of me. My name is Harold Smith, I'm... well I'm a scout for the Boston Red Hawks."

"The Red Hawks", Kaylee asked with a. Sense of wonder in her voice, pretending that she didn't know who he was already and why he was there.

"Oh yes, the Red Hawks. I must say, I was very impressed by your performance today."

"Thank you,", Kaylee said, slightly smiling.

This was it, the moment of truth. Was this Mr. Smith going to invite her to the minors? Or maybe even the majors? Come on, that's too far fetched. But she had to act professional, though at the same time, contain her excitement.

"You ever considered playing with the big guys?" Smith asked with a casual tone, hoping she'd make this easy for him.

"I don't know. Think I could do it?" Kaylee responded. She had never for once doubted herself and in an interview, would probably claim to be better than all the boys.

"Well, we'll never know until you try now, will we?"

"So, what are you saying?"

"I would love to extend an invitation for you to come down to our majors team."

Kaylee's eyes widened in disbelief and excitement, her heart pounding with a mixture of shock and elation. Straight to the majors? Not even an associate team, but the Red Hawks themselves? This was a dream come true and a once in a lifetime opportunity that she had never dared to imagine possible.

"Straight to the major league? That doesn't happen often does it?"

"Hmm. No, but we're willing to try at draft time. And I must say, everything my boss has said about you is true...and more so."

"Your boss?" Kaylee asked bewildered. She assumed that meant the club owner, but to think that any of them had been paying attention..."

Mr. Smith looked a little sheepish, almost as if he had slipped up and revealed something he wasn't supposed to.

"Err.... Yes, have you heard of Elton Mock?"

The name sounded familiar to Kaylee, but she wasn't sure, having not paid attention to that sort of thing, being more focused on the sport of baseball itself. She shook her head to indicate that she didn't.

"Yes, well... Mr. Mock is a tech billionaire, and is the majority owner of several large companies, and this includes the Boston Red Hawks. He personally asked I that I come to watch you play today, and after seeing what I saw, I can see why."

"Well... I'm flattered", Kaylee responded. "But that is hardly believable"

"No really, he asked for you by name"

"Mr. Mock, a tech billionaire and the team owner of the Boston Red Hawks asked for me, Kaylee Dyer, by name, come on." she replies with a sudden chuckle.

"I assure you he did. He has a flare for new talent and really doesn't care about the buzz it'll bring. Plus you're really good, I've seen it myself."

"Speaking of the buzz... there will be a lot of it. Are you sure the Red Hawks are prepared for that?"

"I assure you Kaylee, that is the good kind of buzz, the type everyone needs."

Kaylee wanted this, she had dreamt of this her whole life and was only trying to make it seem like she wasn't desperate, while she prayed inside her that he wouldn't get pissed off at her indecisiveness and leave. Well, the team owner did ask for her by name so he wasn't going anywhere. The team owner believed in her, or so she had been told, but she still needed to know if the scout did.

"I don't know. It's big players out there. I'm not special or anything." Kaylee said almost quietly.

"Ah, but you are Ms. Dyer, you are. You're a kid with a passion, and not only a passion for the sport, but a talent, and the drive. Now, I'm not asking you to join the team now. We still have two weeks left of the season, and we still have to go through the formal bidding process at the draft. But I would still love to offer you a place. That is, if you want it."

"Mr. Smith, thank you, that means a lot. I've dreamed about this day since I was five, and to have it happen so suddenly is... well a lot to take in. Could I get back to you, I need some time to think?"

No she didn't!

"Of course, here's my card. Take a few days, or even a few weeks if you need, and I'll await your answer." With that, Mr. Smith turned and left, leaving Kaylee alone.

Mr. Smith suddenly stopped in his steps.

"You say you've dreamed about this since you were five?"

"Yeah, or six, I'm not too sure."

"You've wanted to be a baseball player since you were five? Most girls around five just wanna play with tea cups and doll houses. I didn't even know about the game until I was twelve."

"Childish passion I guess." Kaylee said with a sheepish smile.

"That right there, is why you're what you are today. That passion, that is what the game needs. I don't really see what you need to think about. You already did when you were five."

With that, Mr. Smith turns again and walks into a bright porshe parked a stone throw distance away from her. Who knew scouts could afford those things.

Kaylee took his business card and placed it in her pocket, and slowly walked back into the locker room. Later that night, she would call Mr. Smith back at the number he gave her, and confirmed her decision. She would love to join the team. She really didn't have to think it through.

That December during the draft lottery, Kaylee found herself in utter disbelief when the Red Hawks selected her as their first draft pick. The news sent shock waves throughout the sports world, sparking a frenzy of media attention and speculation.

Now here she was, standing in the bullpen of Red Hawks stadium.

The stadium was massive, the biggest in the league. It sat 80,000, and was the most modern. Kaylee could only marvel at it, and the other players seemed to share her awe, though the veteran players had been here before, so this was not new for them. As she stepped onto the stage to face a barrage of flashing cameras and eager reporters, Kaylee couldn't help but feel a surge of pride at the historic moment she was a part of.

The press conference that followed was a whirlwind of questions and scrutiny, with journalists clamoring for the chance to interview the trailblazing athlete who managed to be the first draft of the Red Hawks in Boston. Microphones were thrust in Kaylee's direction as reporters fired off questions about her journey to the majors and what it meant to be the first woman to play baseball at such a prestigious level, at least the first not caused by World War Two.

Amidst the chaos, Kaylee remained poised and confident, her responses measured and thoughtful as she fielded inquiries about the challenges she had faced and the obstacles she had overcome.

"It's an honor to be here today," she said, her voice steady despite her nerves that threatened to betray her. "I've worked hard to get to this point, and I'm grateful for the opportunity to represent not only myself but also all the young girls there who dream of playing baseball."

The team manager bends towards the camera.

"Any questions for the lady."

The scrutiny and criticism were nothing new to Kaylee. She had anticipated the backlash that would accompany her groundbreaking achievement, but she refused to let it deter her. If anything, it only fueled her determination to succeed and prove her doubters wrong.

Kaylee points at a well dressed woman in a finely made lady suit.

"Have you ever at any moment doubted that this decision to add a woman to the team is a good one?" the reporter asked.

"Uh... No, I believe that I am as good as a lot of the players out there. I believe I have a lot to offer and I will do just that and more." Kaylee replied with a pois stance.

A lot of reporters begin to throw their hands up again and yell for attention, Kaylee however points at a bearded man in a trench coat. The reporter jumps to his feet.

"Kent Harvey, of the Boston Channel. I just want to know, and I think a lot of people will want to know this too. Don't you think, in your disposition as a woman, that women shouldn't be playing in involved in a heavy sport like baseball with heavy men in the same field. Do you not feel that what you should be advocating for, should be a separate baseball league for women?"

Kaylee turns to look at the team manager who immediately turned his face to the side, letting her face her situation. She breathes a slow sigh.

"I believe that women and men are equal, even if not in size or strength, but in skill. I believe that these matters shouldn't be considered by such methods as is your thinking but by the commitment and the measured skill that both men and women display for the game. And I believe that I will also be an example of this. Thank you. No more questions."

As Kaylee stood in the bullpen of the Red Hawks stadium, surrounded by the towering walls of the massive arena, she couldn't help but feel a sense of awe. The stadium was a testament to the grandeur of the sport she loved, its sprawling stands and state of the art facilities a far cry from the humble ballparks of her youth.

But amidst the awe-inspiring spectacle of the empty stadium, it was Kaylee herself, amongst her team mates, that commanded attention. Her mere presence on the field was a statement- a declaration of her unwavering dedication and unyielding determination to shatter barriers and redefine what it meant to be a baseball player. And as she prepared to take her place among the ranks of the Red Hawks, Kaylee knew that she was ready to make history.

Later that day, Kaylee had gone out to the stadium again to see it in its emptiness. It seemed smaller now, but still majestic in its structure. She marveled once again at the beauty and the size of the stadium. The sight of the modern equipment she was now going to be training with was still baffling.

"So you're the new girl right", a gruff voice said. Kaylee recognized that voice, as it was that of Daryl Rogers, the Red Hawks Short Stop. He was an older man, 36 years old, and a 6 foot 2 inches tall 180 pounds. His dark hair was balding, and his beard was unkempt, though this was a look that he cultivated, and he was known for it.

"Daryl Rogers?" Kaylee asked, mesmerized by being in the presence of who she considered as one of the greats.

"That's the name, don't wear it out. Now are you the new girl, or just a lost fan?" Daryl Royce sounded annoyed, but Kaylee wasn't sure why. Maybe it was because it was her, the first woman ever to join the Major Leagues, but then again, maybe she was just reading too much into it. She had never known his character, or that of any member of the team, but she hoped they smiled as much as she saw on television.

"Yes, I'm the new girl", Kaylee said, not wanting to let his attitude bother her. "Kaylee Dyer."

Kaylee stretches her hand for a handshake. Daryl stares at the hand, then fumes, refusing to pay attention to it.

"Hmm, yeah", Daryl said as he looked over his new teammate. "I see why they picked you."

Kaylee pulls back her tired hand, not too surprised by his attitude. She had come to expect all of this and only hoped that the others wouldn't be like this.

"And why is that?"

"Your looks will certainly get the ratings."

Kaylee's face paled.

"I'm sorry?"

"You and I both know why you're really here!" Daryl spat out.

"I'm sorry," Kaylee said honestly once again, "I thought it was to play baseball. It is to play baseball right?"

"Don't give me that shit", Daryl said with a vigor. "They only picked you for your looks and as a check mark on their woke bingo card."

Kaylee looked hurt at this, but tried to take it in stride.

"Daryl, I know people may have an issue with a female playing baseball, but I am a baseball player, and a damn good one. I've got a 2.20 ERA in college and a batting average of ..."

"I don't care what those numbers say," Daryl spat out. "As far as I'm concerned you got those numbers for one reason, and one reason only." The man's eyes then drifted down, this did not go unnoticed by Kaylee.

"What is wrong with you?", Kaylee demanded, starting to lose her cool. "You have no idea what I've been through to get here, the hours of training, and you dare stand there and insult me like this?"

Daryl scoffed. "Oh shut the hell up," Daryl spat out, "You're a bonus pick..."

"I'm pretty sure I'm the first pick," Kaylee interrupted.

"Nobody gives a shit about that. That fucking billionaire wants to make a name and what better way to make everyone like him than adding a hot woman to the team, because that just seems to please everyone these days."

Kaylee cursed him under her breath. He couldn't possible be right. Right?

"I am a base..."

"Enjoy your time here girly. It ain't gonna last long, and I for one can't wait to see you crash and burn." The man than spat on the ground, turned and walked away without saying another word, leaving Kaylee standing in silence.

"I see you met Daryl", another voice said, one which Kaylee also recognized as Mel Schwartz, catcher for the Red Hawks.

"Yeah, it's... not what I expected?"

"Yeah that's Daryl, don't let him get to you. He's an asshole to everyone, and I think he was more shocked to see a female player than he was to find out he has a bad back."

Kaylee chuckled, despite the situation.

"Bad back? Is he not fit to play?"

"Oh no, he's still fine, but the guy has a complex, and a chip on his shoulder."

"What do you mean?"

"He's been a player for 8 years, and he's always felt that the media has never given him his proper credit. He's a solid player, a good fielder, and can hit, but has never been able to get that ring from the World Series. Which is funny, seeing that he plays for one of the biggest teams in the country. Then you come along, and get all the attention, well I think it was just too much for him."

"I didn't mean to...." Kaylee stuttered.

"I know, and he knows it too. He just needs some time. You'll see, the moment you go out there and kick ass, he'll change his tune. Or at least I hope."

"Well, I'm just grateful someone was nice to me on my first day."

Mel could feel the sarcasm in her tone as she turned again to look at Daryl's direction.

"Hey, it's what teammates do, right?"

Kaylee nodded.

"Anyway, let me show you around."

And so, Mel took her on a tour of the stadium. The first stop was the dugout, and the locker rooms, and then the bullpen, where she then met more members of the team. Aside from Daryl, they all seemed receptive of her.

"Hey there", another voice said, a rather deep one at that. It was that of Mark Watt, a third baseman for the Red Hawks. "You're the newbie aren't ya?"

"Err.. yes, Kaylee Dyer. Pleasure to meet you."

Mark took her hand and shook it, and the two looked at each other. Kaylee noted he was handsome, with short blonde hair, and a very athletic build.

"Well Ms. Dyer, it is a pleasure to meet you. I have to say, you've already caused quite a stir."

"Have I now", Kaylee asked, trying not to sound nervous, despite how attractive this man was. If she wasn't so professional, she would have fallen heads over heels for the man.

"Indeed. You've stirred up quite a commotion in the sports community. You know the internet has been on fire, ever since the news broke."

"Yeah, I've seen the posts", Kaylee said, a hint of sadness in her voice. "Some are more kind than others, but I think it comes with the territory. It was bound to happen. I'm not just some ordinary female after all, I'm a baseball player."

"True", Mark replied. "Though some of the more vocal people on the internet need a good slap. There are some that are very welcoming of the idea, and some not so much."

"That's true. Though, I'm sure the owners will get a huge boost in attendance."

"Yeah, rumor is old Elton asked for you personally. Is that true?" Mark asked, raising an eyebrow.

"As far as I know. That is what the recruiter said when we first met. He seemed a bit embarrassed to have admitted that though."

Mark whistled at this. "Color me impressed. Well, I can't wait to share some victories with you." With that Mark turned and left.

"He seems nice."

"Yes, he is", Mel replied. "A real gentle giant. You couldn't ask for a better teammate, and the ladies love him... even if he is married."

Shit! There goes her chance.

"I just wish we had more Mark's and less Daryl's."

Mel laughed at this. "Me too kid, me too."

The rest of the day went by rather quickly, and Kaylee got to meet the rest of the team. She didn't get to meet Mr. Mock though since he didn't actually live in the Boston area. Once she returned to her apartment, save for one individual, she was looking forward to fulfilling her dream.

Chapter 2
Secrets and Confrontations

In the ensuing weeks, Kaylee's schedule became consumed with a different kind of preparation, paperwork. Mountains of it in fact, enough to rival the tallest skyscrapers in Boston. There were liability waivers, medical forms, contracts, and more legal jargon than she could have imagined. She almost thought she saw something about life insurance. Each page seemed to blur into the next, a never-ending maze of bureaucratic red tape that threatened to suffocate her with its sheer monotony.

Despite the mind-numbing nature of the task, Kaylee soldiered on, her determination unwavering even in the face of a paperwork induced despair. She knew that every signature brought her one step closer to her dream, and that was motivation enough to keep pushing forward.

But as the days dragged on and the paperwork continued to pile up, Kaylee found herself growing increasingly frustrated with one person in particular, Daryl. Their strained relationship had only worsened in recent weeks, his hostility towards her seemingly escalating with each passing day. While the rest of the team had welcomed her with open arms, Daryl remained an unwavering source of tension and hostility.

Despite the challenges she faced, Kaylee found solace in the prospect of spring training. The thought of finally stepping onto the field with her teammates and competing against other professional teams filled her with a renewed sense of excitement and anticipation. It was a chance to prove herself on the biggest stage, to show the world what she was capable of and silence her doubters once and for all.

And so, it was a mixture of nerves and excitement that Kaylee boarded the plane bound for Florida for spring training, her teammates and the team manager by her side. The private charter, courtesy of Mr. Mock, was a luxurious touch that spoke to the prestige of the Red Hawks organization. As the plane soared through the clouds, Kaylee couldn't help but feel a sense of awe at the journey that lay ahead.

Despite the lingering tension with Daryl and her own insecurities about her size compared to her teammates, Kaylee refused to let the doubt creep in. She was here for a reason, she reminded herself, a reason that went beyond paperwork and politics. And as she gazed out the window at the vast expanse of sky stretching out before her, Kaylee felt a surge of determination wash over her. No matter what challenges lay ahead, she was ready to face them head-on. Or so she told herself.

"So, Ms. Dyer, are you ready to go?" This came from the team manager, John Gleason. He was an older man, in his 60's, and a grizzled veteran of the field. He had moved from his seat to the one next to Kaylee.

"Oh yes sir, I'm excited and ready to go. This is the chance of a lifetime."

"Hmm, yes, it is. Now, you realize we are going to have to make some adjustments. It's not just the media that is going to have an issue, but the opposing team as well. They are going to be looking for any opportunity to take advantage."

"I've had to do this my entire life," Kaylee replied nonchalantly. "And quite a bit more recently too," she added as she glanced at Daryl who refused to even look her direction.

"Well, I see you've met Daryl," John whispers. "Take it easy on the lad okay, he's had a rough few years."

"Eight years of not having a ring after a bad back and all that effort, doesn't seem like a few years to me."

"Well, I'm already glad you understand."

"That still doesn't give him the right to be mad at everyone else. We're teammates, we're supposed to be working together. I mean if we can't be close, who else can?"

"I don't know, spouses. Rich people maybe."

Kaylee did not laugh at this, quite contrary to what John hoped would happen.

"Anyways just, be cool about him. He's hard on himself, and everyone else, but he's got a good heart when he needs to."

"I'm not here for him anyway. I'm here to do me."

"Hmm, yes", John muttered. "You have a good head on your shoulders Dyer, and a strong work ethic. I can tell, and I think we can make this work. Just uh... don't just do you, yeah? Let's try to do the whole team. That will work."

"I sure hope so", Kaylee said, hoping she could make a good impression.

"Good, because you're the starting pitcher at first game." John announced, hiding his emotions, wanting to see how Kaylee responded.

"Really?!" Kaylee gasped, her face lighting up. "I was hoping to play, but as a starter? That's great."

John laughed at her reaction and gave her a smile. "Good you're the last one on the team I've told this to, and all of them are excited to see what you got, well save for one."

Daryl let out a humph at this.

"Here is the full roster for the game. Break a leg. Not literally of course" Gleesom then got up and returned to his seat on the plane.

Kaylee looked down at the paper in front of her and read through the lineup. She had a few familiar names on there, Mark Watt, and Mel Schwartz, but then there were some names of teammates she was less familiar with. She supposed she would get to know them over training, that was the whole point, right?

Kaylee was in a good mood for the remainder of the trip. Even Daryl's attitude towards her did not deter her from her goal.

As the plane descended towards the sun-kissed shores of Florida, Kaylee's heart raced with anticipation. The sight of palm tree's swaying in the gentle breeze and sparkling waters stretching out towards the horizon, filled her with a sense of wonder. This was her first time in Florida, and she couldn't help but marvel at the beauty that surrounded her.

As the team disembarked from the plane, they were greeted by the warm embrace of the Florida sun and the welcoming smiles of their teammates and Red Hawks staff. It was a moment of camaraderie and excitement, a shared sense of anticipation for the journey that lay ahead.

As they made their way to the hotel, Kaylee's eyes darted eagerly around, taking in the sights and sounds of their new surroundings. The vibrant colors of exotic flowers, the rhythmic sway of palm fronds, and the distant sound of waves crashing against the shore, it was a sensory overload that left her breathless with excitement.

Upon arriving at the hotel, Kaylee was struck by its grandeur. The lobby was a masterpiece of marble floors, towering columns, and plush furnishing, a testament to the luxury that awaited them. As she followed her teammates through the elegant corridors, she couldn't help but feel a sense of awe at the opulence that surrounded her.

As they reached their rooms, Kaylee's heart fluttered with excitement. Opening the door, she was greeted by a scene of pure luxury, a king-sized bed adorned with soft, fluffy pillows, a spacious sitting area with plush armchairs, and a balcony overlooking the sparkling pool below.

Sinking down onto the bed, Kaylee let out a contented sigh, the weight of the day's events finally catching up with her. As she closed her eyes and let the warmth of the Florida sun wash over her, she felt a sense of peace settle over her. Tomorrow would bring new challenges and new opportunities, but for now, she allowed herself to simply savor the moment and bask in the excitement of the journey that lay ahead. She laid down and was about to shut her eyes when she suddenly remembered, she needed to shower.

———•———

THE NEXT DAY AT THE stadium came by much faster than expected, and Kaylee was nervous. They weren't playing any other teams today, just them and the reserves. However, even if it wasn't an exposition game with another team, it was still her first real public major league game that she was playing, and she knew that today would cement for many how they thought of her. No pressure.

"Hey Dyer", Mel called out, getting her attention. "I hope you're ready."

"I'm ready", Kaylee replied. "I've trained hard for this."

"You may have trained hard, but you still have never played against real players before, and no the college level doesn't count."

"I understand that, and I will do my best. I just have to focus and ignore the rest. It will be easy."

"If you say so." Mel replied, though his tone showed doubt. They then headed out into the diamond, with Kaylee going to the pitch. They would be fielding first.

The first person up was none other than Daryl himself, and Kaylee felt her heart drop. Of course, it had to be him! He had a look on his face as if he was ready to murder someone, and she knew it was her specifically. He stared daggers at her, and spat on the ground before lifting up his bat. She couldn't get this wrong, she needed to prove herself, to inspire others.

The anticipation hung thick in the air as the players and spectators alike watched with bated breath, their eyes fixed on the showdown unfolding before them. Kaylee's heart pounded in her chest as she watched Daryl fix a stern stance on the plate, his expression a mask of hard aggression mixed with a fixed frown. She knew that this was her chance to prove herself, to show the world what she was made of.

As Mel signaled for the first pitch, Kaylee felt a surge of adrenaline course through her veins. She wound up her arm and released the ball with all the force she could muster, sending it hurtling towards the plate with lightning speed. The coaches and spectators watched, hardly able to keep a steady look at the ball as it rushed towards the man with the bat. Daryl swung the bat with all his might, but the ball sailed past him, leaving him empty handed and frustrated.

"Strike one!" the umpire called out, his voice cutting through the tension like a knife. Kaylee allowed herself a small smile of satisfaction, knowing that she had caught Daryl off guard with her speed and accuracy. And worst, with a lot of spectators watching, a lot of Daryl's fans too.

But Daryl was not one to back down so easily. As Kaylee prepared to throw her next pitch, she could see the fire burning in his eyes, his determination to best her evident for all to see. She released the ball once more, and once again, Daryl swung and missed.

"Strike two!" the umpire declared, his voice ringing out across the field. Kaylee could feel the tension mounting with each passing moment, the weight of the moment pressing down on her like a lead weight.

"Fuck off, girly," Daryl growled, his frustration boiling over as he lashed out at Kaylee. But she refused to be intimidated, meeting his gaze with steely determination. However, she resolved to be cool about it.

"I'm sorry?" Kaylee responded.

"Don't you play dumb with me! I'm the real talent here, not you."

"You sure are, I mean you did just miss two swings in a row, but whatever", Kaylee called out. It was hard to tell behind his mask, but she was pretty sure Mel was smiling.

"Why don't you take your fast ball throwing ass to your sugar daddy Mock, that's how you got here in the first place isn't it?" Daryl spat out suddenly.

"The hell did you say to me?" Kaylee responded with an angry tone, an anger that was beginning to rise first in her.

"What are you gonna do, fight me? You shouldn't even be seeing me. This place is for players, not women who got here cuz they're cute."

"Fuck you Daryl."

"Nah fuck you!"

"Hey, knock it off! I'm not gonna have that here. We all came here to practice and that's what we're gonna do. At least keep your stupid talk to yourselves, not in front of these people." the umpire interjected, his voice stern as he reprimanded Daryl for his outburst. The crowd murmured in disapproval, their eyes narrowing on the disgraced player who had let his temper get the best of him.

Undeterred, Kaylee focused her attention on the task at hand. With one final deep breath, she wound up for her pitch and released the ball with all her might. Time seemed to slow to a crawl as the ball soared through the air, its trajectory guided by Kaylee's skill and determination.

And then, in a moment that seemed to defy all logic, the ball found its mark, landing squarely in the catcher's mitt with a satisfying thud. The umpire's call rang out across the field, sealing Daryl's fate with three simple words.

"Strike three, you're out!"

A roar of triumph erupted from the crowd as Kaylee stood on the mound, her chest heaving with exertion and pride. She had done it, she had struck out one of the top players on the team, proving once and for all that she belonged on the field with the best of them. She wished she could have another interview at that moment so she could laugh in the faces of the reporters. Alas, this was only the beginning, and the game had to go on.

As Daryl stormed off the plate in a fit of rage, Kaylee couldn't help but feel a sense of satisfaction wash over her. She had silenced her doubters and made her mark on the game, at least for now, but it was a moment she would cherish for years to come. And as she watched the next batter step up to the plate, she knew that this was only the beginning and as of now she suddenly felt more prepared than she had ever been.

The next two players of the inning turned up on the plate, grabbing the metal bat with precision and fixing a stern stance, indicating that they were ready and were not going out like the last guy. WHAM! WHAP! The ball kept falling into the catchers mitt and they all ended up as full strikeouts as well. Kaylee had never felt more triumphant before. It was all coming together. It wasn't over, but it had started well. It was now their turn to hit.

As the inning progressed, Kaylee watched with a mix of excitement and nerves as her teammates stepped up to the plate, each one carrying a strong will to make their mark on the game. The crack of the bat and the roar of the small crowd filled the air as hits and misses alike echoed across the field.

When it was finally Kaylee's turn to hit, she felt a surge of anticipation coursing through her veins. Even if she wasn't going first this time, that would be far to on the nose. Instead she watched Mel take home and his turn to hit, which he did successfully. Mark was right behind him and made it look easy.

Then it was Kaylee's turn. This was her moment to shine, her chance to prove herself on the field. But as she stepped up to the plate, she couldn't shake the butterflies fluttering in her stomach.

"Break a leg out there," the coach for her practice team said, offering her a reassuring pat on the shoulder. He hesitated for a moment, realizing his mistake in using a physical touch, but Kaylee simply waved him off with a smile. She was used to the occasional slip-up, and she knew that his words were meant to encourage her.

Taking a deep breath, Kaylee focused her gaze on the pitcher, a burly looking man, who stood a good foot taller than her. Embarrassingly, she hadn't memorized his name yet as he was on the reserve and didn't spend a lot of time with them, the mainline players. She wondered if he dreaded her too, seeing that she came in as a woman and went straight to the major league and is now a mainline player, a position he had worked hard for and is still working hard for. Anyway, she would need to get a hit off of him, and quickly.

Kaylee gripped the bat tightly in her hands, the weight of it familiar and comforting. She didn't have to wait long as the pitch was thrown, a curve ball, which came at her at the speed of light. With a swift motion, she swung the bat with all her might, the satisfying thud of the ball connecting with the bat ringing out across the field. It connected with a crack, and the ball soared high in the air, and it was a near home run. She dropped her bat and began to jog the diamond along with Mel and Mark, all the while Daryl on the field was giving her glares the entire time. As she sprinted towards first base, Kaylee felt a surge of adrenaline coursing through her veins. The crowd erupted into cheers, their voices mingling with the sound of her own heartbeat pounding in her ears. She rounded first base with ease, her eyes locked on the ball as it sailed through the air, landing safely in the outfield.

But Kaylee wasn't content to stop at first base. With the determination burning in her chest, she dug deep and pushed herself to keep running, her legs pumping with every ounce of strength she had. The outfielders scrambled to retrieve the ball, but Kaylee was already halfway to second base, her eyes fixed on the prize.

As she slid into second base with a triumphant grin, Kaylee felt a surge of pride swell within her. She had done it, she had made it to second base, proving once and for all that she could hold her own on the field, and play with the best of them. Daryl who was watching attentively the whole time, waiting for an error from the lady, turned to the side with a growl.

The crowd erupted into cheers as Kaylee stood on second base, her chest heaving with exertion and pride. She glanced back at her teammates, their faces alight with excitement and admiration. They knew what this meant, that Kaylee was here to stay and that she was a force to be reckoned with on the baseball diamond. She was definitely too hard for softball.

For the rest of the game, Kaylee kept giving strikeout after strikeout, and from this front achieved a perfect game with no hits. It was perhaps the best game she had ever played. She had less luck with her hitting record, and did miss a few pitches and did get a few strikeouts, but what fun would it be without that?

She was happy when the game was over, her team had won. The players shook hands and fist bumped each other, both winners and losers. It was all together a good practice.

The crowd had started to retreat, having been satisfied with the performance of the woman who wouldn't stop smiling over her win. But her joy would not last. The moment the game was over, and the teams were heading back to the locker rooms, Daryl cornered her.

"You think you're funny huh," Daryl said with a cold anger, the hate that rested in his eyes evident.

"I'm sorry what?", Kaylee asked.

"Don't play dumb with me. You think you're the shit don't you? Just because you were able to pitch a single game, and a lucky one at that, you're already above everyone else aren't ya?"

"I don't know what you're talking about. I'm pretty sure I've been acting perfectly normal"

"Bullshit", Daryl said with a venom. Stamping his fist into the wall band her. A drop of sweat fell of Kaylee's head.

"Listen, Daryl," Kaylee had finally mustered the confidence to speak back. "I'm just here to play baseball and I really don't care if it pleases you or not. I wish we were cool but since you're so persistent in putting an effort to make sure that doesn't happen, then we'll leave it that way. But don't you dare try to make it look like I am a threat to your career. I'm just here to play baseball."

"Yeah, but aren't you worried about how you got here?" Daryl replied, his tone now tamed but still conniving.

"Does it really matter? I'm here, aren't I?"

Daryl chuckles and goes ahead to add an evil humph.

"You have no idea. You know nothing about these rich people. They never give anything for free. You're not special Dyer, you're not different, and you're damn sure not better than anyone else either. He'll come for you when he wants what he wants, you know that right? One day, could be anytime now."

"I don't believe you. You just don't want me here. Well, guess what Daryl, I'm here to stay, with or without your approval."

"You staying here, depends on one thing. But are you willing to give that thing?"

Kaylee remains silent, hoping that her thoughts weren't simultaneous with his statement.

"No, you're not," Daryl added. "You ain't special girl. You're just another person they're gonna use."

Oh hell no! What does he mean by that?

"What do you mean by that?" Kaylee final spoke out in an inquisitive tone.

"Hey, what's going on here?" A loud deep voice said. Both Kaylee and Daryl turned to see the big burly pitcher from earlier. "What do you think you're doing Roger's?"

"Just.... congratulating our new player on a perfect game, Daryl said methodically and slowly. He then turned and walked away, all under the glare of the pitcher. Kaylee was grateful for the rescue but wished for a second that the figure had delayed a little.

"Thanks...uh.... I'm sorry, I haven't remembered your name yet."

The pitcher chuckled.

"Don't worry, you're new. My name is John Marx, but my friends call me little John."

"Little John?", Kaylee questioned.

"Yeah, like little John and Robin Hood. For the same reason, it's meant to be ironic. Plus, I like it, so...."

"Oh, I'm not criticizing any of that", Kaylee said, raising her hands defensively. "It kinda suits you."

"I'll work with kinda."

Little John smiled at her. He was a rather big and muscular guy, standing well over six feet and built like a mountain, which put more irony into the name 'Little John'. He also had a voice like the sound of pure bass. He was wearing a sleeveless shirt, which exposed his rather large and bulging arms, which was a bit intimidating, yet his personality was sweet, which gave less irony to the name 'Little John'. But he was defiantly a gentle giant.

"You did pretty well out there, better than I have to say, and I was the one that was supposed to have the perfect game."

"Thank you. I know it was a lucky strike, and I've trained hard."

"That's all a matter of opinion. You were good, and you should be proud of it. Not everyone can have a perfect game."

"I have to agree with Little John here", a voice called out, which was Mel. "What you did out there, requires raw talent, and you have that. I'd say if you even showed half... no twenty five percent of what you did today, I'd say you have a bright career ahead of you."

"You think so?" Kaylee asked slightly bewildered.

"Absolutely." Mel said, and patted her on the back.

"Well, I'm going to shower. It was great meeting you", Little John said, and gave her a firm handshake, his hand engulfing hers, and walked away. Mel soon did the same, leaving Kaylee alone with her thoughts.

———◉———

KAYLEE'S GRAND-SLAM

KAYLEE WOKE UP THE next day feeling strong and hearty. The softness of the bed brought a comfortable feel to her body, which was a huge necessity for her. She already imagined the days activities... hit the gym with the dudes, sweat off a little muscle, head to practice without the thought of freshening up and play as good as the day before. She had expected that today, everyone would be at their best, especially Daryl who would definitely try to down press her in some way. She had stayed up for over an hour thinking about their conversation and how it ended. What did he mean by 'was she willing to give?'. Even though she tried to not let it bother her, somehow it wouldn't stop dancing in her head. She hoped and prayed that everything Daryl said was just to discourage her. She hoped even more that there isn't something she'd have to give to remain on the team.

Kaylee ordered food and went in for a shower. She took her time, seeing that she had woken up early, probably before everyone else. By the time she was out of the bathroom, the food was already waiting for her. She dressed up and had a light meal then headed out at a time she felt everyone else would be out.

Upon arriving to the stadium, Kaylee was surprised to find that the training for the day had been canceled. That was certainly odd, and it certainly wasn't for weather, it was beautiful outside with no storms in the forecast.

"Hey anyone know why the game was canceled today?" Kaylee asked aloud.

"Maybe you embarrassed the other team too much yesterday and they don't want to show their faces?" Mel suggested with a laugh.

Kaylee was about to say something, when another familiar voice cut in. It was Little John, who had just entered the locker room.

"Hey, the TM wants to see you Dyer. It's actually about the canceled game that you're complaining about."

"Me?" Kaylee asked. "What did I do? I didn't ask for the game to be canceled."

"Don't know. Apparently the request came from Mr. Mock himself", Little John continued.

"Really", Kaylee replied in astonishment. Why would the owner ask for her specifically? She hadn't even met him yet. Her mind quickly raced back to her conversation with Daryl. She swerved her eyeballs around the room to find him but he was absent. Kaylee hoped that this wasn't true, it couldn't be. She waved it off.

"Hey, I don't make the rules", Little John said, interrupting her thoughts. "I just follow them. If the owner asks for you, and the coach says go, well then I guess you better go."

With all things said and done, Kaylee departed the room for the coach's spring training office and knocked.

"Come in", the familiar voice called out. Kaylee followed the directions as requested and entered and was surprised to find that Daryl was also in the room.

"Kaylee, good, glad you made it", Team Manager John Gleesom said, as if he had invited her here. "I wanted to discuss something with you and Rogers here."

"Ok." Both of them said at the same time, much to Daryl's annoyance.

"Mr. Mock has requested that you both meet him at his home in Naples, one county down from here."

"Meet.... Mr. Mock?" Kaylee said surprised. "As in the club owner? At his home?"

"At his Spring home more specifically." Gleesom corrected.

"But why us, I'm sure he has better things to do than meet us."

"He has something he wants to discuss with both of you.... in person. Some sort of proposition, i'm sure. Two limos are waiting outside for both of you."

"But why cancel training for the whole day?" Kaylee asked. For the first time, it looks like Daryl agreed with her on a point.

TM Gleesom shrugged his shoulders. "Beats me, but what the owner wants, the owner gets....so....."

They remained seated, watching the coach type away on his computer and arrange sheets he was recording from. Gleesom stopped, realizing that they were both still in the room. He pushed the papers to the side, cleared his throat and gave them a suspecting glare.

"You don't like limos or...?" Gleesom echoed.

"Oh you want us to go right now?" Daryl replied.

"No of course not," Gleesom echoed at both of them with an expressionless face. "The cars are just parked outside for decoration, you know. Mock likes to advertise his latest luxuries."

For a moment, Kaylee and Daryl still remain on the spot. Then it hits Kaylee before the short stop realizes.

"Oh, you're being sarcastic," Kaylee says with wide eyes.

Kaylee couldn't complain, and from the look of it, neither could Daryl. They soon both got up and walked outside, where there indeed where the limo's waiting for them, one for each.

The two made their way to their respective limos and began the drive to Elton Mock's house.

———— ◉ ————

THE DRIVE TO SEE MR. Mock was uneventful, and Kaylee found herself in the back of a limo and was quite nervous. She had never ridden in one, and her first time was hardly exciting. It was just a long car anyway. Besides, her mind was hardly on the good life she was living at the time. What could the owner possibly want to talk to her about, let alone Daryl? Still, what the boss wanted, the boss got.

As the limo's pulled into the property of Mr. Mock, Kaylee couldn't help but feel a mixture of both being impressed and intimidated at the same time. The man owned some serious money, that was for sure.

The mansion was enormous, and was easily 100 times bigger than her apartment. The main house itself was three stories tall, and the outside was covered in white stone. The front garden was enormous but still nicely cut. It was designed in a renaissance type of style. There were half a dozen cars parked at the front yard around a large water fountain that was molded into the shape of a lion that held a staff of fire. It looked a bit out of place in the Florida environment, but Kaylee figured that once you were rich enough, that sort of thing no longer mattered. There was a circular driveway, and several people were walking around.

Both of the limos parked, and both Daryl and Kaylee exited. They were both greeted by a servant, a rather young woman.

"Hello, and welcome. My name is Jennifer, and I will be your guide. Would either of you care for a glass of champagne, or anything else?"

Kaylee declined while Daryl gladly accepted both. She kept her eyes up and around, forgetting her concerns, she was filled with astonishment. She however felt that the number of cars was just too much for a mansion he hardly lived in. Soon they headed inside, where they were directed to a sitting room. Kaylee didn't have long to wait however, and a short time later, the door opened, and Elton Mock himself entered the room. He was a portly, but not obese man, standing at about five foot eight. He was wearing a dark blue suit, was clean shaven, and seemed to be balding.

"Elton Mock" he introduced himself, shaking hands with Kaylee, and giving a side acknowledgment to Daryl. "You're probably wondering why I requested both of you?"

Kaylee simply raised an eyebrow, trying not to look annoyed at losing practice for the day, while Daryl's expression did not betray his emotions, he simply didn't care. This couldn't possibly be bad for him.

"I'm sure both of you are familiar with the concept of sexual harassment", Mr. Mock began, and took a seat across from them.

"Yes sir, I'm familiar with the concept", Kaylee replied.

"Well, my dear, it would appear we have a situation here. It would seem, that a certain individual is not being cooperative with the team, and as such, I had to cancel practice for the day so as to.... correct this."

"And?" Daryl replied, taking another sip of champagne.

"And, it would seem that it was the first time we had a perfect game since the 80's, exposition, league or practice games included, and it was because of Ms. Dyer here. Am I correct?

"Well I'd say it was a team effort," Kaylee responded with a shy smile.

"It's baseball, Ms. Dyer, it's hardly ever a team effort," Mock responded. "You my good friend, are a star. You are what this team needs. I see you going far Dyer, I see you."

Kaylee's mind was shaken, she suddenly remembered why she may be here.

"I don't know about good friends. We barely know each other."

"However, I heard some rumors about..... your behavior Mr. Roger's." Mock said, turning a stern eye to Daryl who was seated comfortably, enjoying the glass of champagne and getting pissed off by the praises Mock was giving to Kaylee, which he had to listen to.

Daryl froze, and looked down. Maybe it could be bad for him.

"Rumors sir?"

"Indeed, I'm not a fan of these rumors, but it would appear that they are true. Now, normally this wouldn't be an issue, and we could just have a talk, but it would seem the press is interested."

"The press" both Kaylee and Daryl asked at the same time.

"Yes. There have been rumors circulating that a member of the Red Hawks, has been less than friendly to the team's newest female player, and that the rumors may be true. It would certainly look.... bad should they run a story about that. Now of course, there is a remedy." At this two big burly men entered the room and were flanking Daryl.

Daryl stood up at this and looked around. "What the hell is the meaning of this?"

"There is a saying, Mr. Roger's. Fake it till you make it. Well, I'm not about to let your attitude cost me, and I think I have an idea. Mr. Adam's and Mr. Jefferson here will give you a... lesson if you will."

"You can't do this to me. You don't own me."

"I'm sure a million dollar contract would argue with that assumption kid. I do own you, you know why? Because you play for my goddamn team. Not unless you wanna quit?"

Daryl stands breathing hard. He steals a side glance at the two men standing beside him.

"What makes you think I won't?" Daryl spat out.

"Two million in gambling debts, two hundred thousand in medical debt, a couple hundred thousand dollars in insurances and tax debts. I mean tax debts, how do you even get tax debts? You're a goddamn baseball star. I've seen the records kid, you need this team more than it needs you."

"How do you know that?"

"I'm a billionaire, there's not a lot of things that I don't know. If I don't know, then I don't want to know. That's how I stay rich. Now be a good boy, and let the men do their jobs. Let's all just do our best to save the team."

With that, the two burly men picked Daryl up and escorted him out of the room, leaving Mr. Mock and Kaylee by themselves.

Kaylee watched as the drama unfold, completely dumbfounded. She had no idea what they were going to do to him, but she knew it wasn't good. She felt nervous and uncomfortable, even though she was seated on a very comfortable Italian couch.

"What are they gonna do to him?" Kaylee asked in a demanding but soft tone.

"Don't worry about him, let's talk about you," Mr. Mock responded, making sure to deviate the subject. "How's the rest of the team treating you?"

"Well, I guess you already know. You seem to know everything. Luckily, I don't have debts."

Mr. Mock chuckles. "You're an interesting woman Ms. Dyer. Tell me, are you seeing anyone?"

"Not at the moment, no," Kaylee wondered why this information was important. "Why?"

"You know, just asking."

"I'm really concerned about Daryl, should I check on him?"

"I've told you not to worry about him. He'll be fine. He has a limo driving him back. This moment, is just for you and me."

"What do you mean?"

Mr. Mock pours himself a bottle of champagne and moves to sit next to Kaylee, bringing his body annoyingly close to hers.

"I mean, it's just you and me in here. It's our moment."

"Mr. Mock, I'm not sure I understand. What is happening, and why did you bring me here?"

Mr. Mock chuckled. "I've seen the tapes. You're a smart girl. But you are also an attractive one I must say."

Kaylee had a bad feeling about this, and tried to move away from the team owner, but was unsuccessful.

"So, what do you say, my dear? I think we can help each other out."

"I'm sorry what? I'm not sure I understand. You wanted to see me to solve a sex harassment scandal with you, but now you want to create a full-on sex scandal?"

"Don't worry dear. It's all legal, and besides, it will only help our ratings. Don't you want that?"

Kaylee shook her head to gesture 'NO', and tried to get away, but Mr. Mock had an iron grip. "I think you have a misunderstanding on what is legal and what isn't."

Mr. Mock scoffed at this. "Legal? Please. There are many forms of legal. Now, don't worry. It's all consensual."

"Consensual!" Kaylee shouted. "It absolutely is not!"

Mr. Mock looked annoyed at this. "Come now, no need to be hasty..."

"I... uh... I think I should go", Kaylee stammered as she tried to pick up her things.

"Hmm... shame. Why don't you think about it, you know my address. It sure would be a shame if... unpleasant things were to happen to your career over this."

Kaylee froze. Was he really doing this? Did he really just say that?

"Did you just threaten me?" Kaylee asked in a hashed tone. She wondered herself where the confidence came from.

"Ms. Dyer, I own the Red Hawks which you just signed to, just in case you forgot. I hardly need to threaten you."

"So you're going to terminate my contract, which I just started filling, and which was a lot of fucking paperwork by the way, because I refused to sleep with you?" Kaylee yelled. She was now outraged and wasn't afraid to show it.

"Oh, keep your voice down. It's just a mutual agreement. I need you, you need my team. Come on, we're both adults here. You're a young, beautiful woman. You'd probably go to a bar one day, drink a dozen shots and go back home with some accountant from Fed Ex who owns a bike and lives in an apartment in the suburbs."

"I live in the suburbs."

"The point is, you give out sex for free. A lot of the time. Now I'm giving you the chance to do it, and enjoy it by the way, in exchange for something you've wanted your whole life. Come on, you know you want this."

Kaylee remained silent for a while, trying to figure out what to say.

"He was right," Kaylee said in a very muffled tune. "I'm not special. I'm just attractive. You brought me here because you got turned on from seeing a woman on television."

"I'm sorry who was right?" Mr. Mock asked.

"I'm sorry, but I'm not going to do this. It goes against everything I stand for."

"Just think about it", Mr. Mock said, his expression still blank. "You shouldn't rush such decisions, Ms. Dyer."

"I'm... I'm not sure I can do that", Kaylee said honestly.

"Hmm.... shame. Well your limo is waiting outside and will take you back to your hotel. Just think about it, O.K?" Mr. Mock said this with an icy coolness, which said everything about what exactly he meant by that.

"Yes sir." Kaylee said and quickly left, the sound of her heartbeat was deafening in her ears. She wasn't sure what just happened and didn't want to think about it.

KAYLEE'S GRAND-SLAM

The next 30 minutes was a blur, and she could only remember quickly making her way into the limo to get away. She felt tears threatening to roll down her eyes but she fought hard to contain them. The memories of the days events kept hitting hard at her. The next thing she knew, she was back at her hotel. She rushed quickly past everyone and ran up the stairs, avoiding the elevator until she was in her room and locked the door.

Kaylee made her way to the shower, turned it on and just sat there. The water poured down uncontrollably and drenched her in her clothes. She sat there thinking and asking herself questions until she began to cry. Was she never good enough? We're all her years of training and passion a waste of time. Was this the real world? Was everyone like this? Is this what it took to achieve one's dreams? Daryl, it appears, was right about why she was drafted onto the team. God damn it.

Chapter 3
The Reporter

Kaylee probably had the worst nightmare of her life that night. She was fleeing to the limo to escape Mr. Mock as he desperately pursued her, wanting only to get what he wanted. As soon as she got into the car, she heard the door lock. Suddenly a gas came out of the vents and filled the vehicle, no matter how hard she tried, she couldn't fight it, it was gas after all. She was soon knocked unconscious. In the dream, when she woke up again, feeling comfortable and assuming for a split second that she was safe, she turned to witnesses the most unbelievable abomination, she was in bed with Mr. Mock.

She screamed, waking herself up with a startle. She sat up in bed and found her forehead was sweaty and her heart was beating rapidly. Luckily, she was in the warm comforts of her hotel room, now filled with daylight and looking out through the open windows into warm rays of the Florida sun, it always felt as if Florida had its own special sun.

"That was a terrible dream", she muttered. "But a dream nonetheless." Either way, as a result, Kaylee found her self unable to sleep and could only wait for the attached restaurant to the hotel to open for breakfast. It was still very early in the morning and the sun had just begun to rise. Kaylee tried hard to sleep but it just wouldn't happen. She stretched all over the bed, trying to be as comfortable as possible, but achieved no satisfactory result. She tried to read a book, attempted to play video games on her phone, watch some online comedy but the reality would still hit her at every moment. She was extremely relieved when the morning sun came up fully despite her lack of sleep.

The attached diner was owned by a local chain, and she found herself amused it was named Mel's like her catcher. Quite contrary to most people, she found it soothing to see that not a lot of people in the restaurant recognized her as the newest sign in for the Boston Red Hawks, a formidable team in the baseball major league, a team with... 'Who am I kidding, I just started playing.' She walked in briskly, hoping that even the few that did recognize her would stop at their shy waves and not make a scene of it. She definitely couldn't have at this moment, not with all that's going on.

She took a seat and ordered a meal, which arrived shortly, and she began to eat, hoping that the nightmare would not repeat. She would make sure she stayed awake for the whole day and night if she had to. She wasn't even halfway done with her meal when a man approached her table.

"Good morning ma'am, my name is Ed Oakley, I'm a reporter with *Northeast baseball*. Do you mind if I join you? Maybe ask a few questions?"

Oakley? Where had she heard that name before? Besides that, she knew she should refer all reporters to her agent, but something about this guy felt different.

"Sure", Kaylee said with a shrug of her shoulders. "I can answer a few questions. Nothing too deep, I'm sure you can understand, being a reporter and all. I'm not really supposed to answer questions, as that is the job of my agent."

"Yes, yes, of course", Oakley replied. He was a large man, easily over six foot, and had a rather stocky build, and a beard. Funny how virtually everyone she came across was over six foot or close.

"Now, I've heard the rumor about your addition to the team..."

"It's true!", Kaylee said bluntly, remembering her experience with Mr. Mock the day before. She had figured he was coming to ask about that and had already decided to give him a straight answer, she had no strength or time to battle the truth or try to protect the team or managers name. She just wanted to enjoy her meal.

Mr. Oakley looked taken aback by this. "I'm sorry? Don't you want to know what these rumors are that I'm talking about?"

"Let me guess, they were started by Daryl Rogers on why I was drafted to the team? After meeting Mr. Mock, I have to admit he is right."

Mr. Oakley looked horrified at this revelation. "Uh....no, that's not what I was talking about at all. Though what you said sounds more interesting than what I had."

Kaylee cursed under her breath. She still wanted to play baseball, despite Mr. Mock's actions, and really did not want to face his wrath. She needed to find a way to spin this, and fast.

"Yes, well, I'm afraid I have said too much."

"I understand, but please, it will really help me. If you wish it to keep it confidential, I totally understand."

Kaylee did not want to share this part of the story, as she felt that she had no right to do so. But she deeply wished that she could say something to someone, even if said person is a stranger. Besides, it wouldn't hurt to know if sharing the problem with Mr. Oakley would solve half of it.

"All right, but if you print any of this, you're a dead man," Kaylee said, not really knowing how she would make him a dead man if he did go ahead and print it.

"Understood," Mr. Oakley said, raising his hands defensively. "Now then, why don't we get started."

"All right," Kaylee said.

With that, Kaylee began her tale of what had happened yesterday during her visit with Mr. Mock, and what he had tried to do. The entire time as he sat there, Mr. Oakley seemed to get angrier and angrier on her behalf.

"My God," Mr. Oakley said, his voice barely a whisper. "I knew he was a rat bastard, far and away from his public persona, but to do something like this..."

"Yes, but remember, please don't publish this. I have no love lost for the man, but I'm powerless because of what he can do to me.... I just.... needed to get it off my chest." Kaylee's eyes looked downcast and straight up defeated when she said these words. Mr. Oakley could feel that she was truly lost and wished at that moment that he could squeeze life out of Mr. Mock.

"No, no... I completely understand. Not a word will escape my lips. Scouts honor."

"Now... what was that rumor you actually wanted to talk to me about?" Kaylee asked, curious at what he had come to say.

"Hmm, oh yes. Well from what I heard, Mr. Mock wanted to use your hiring to generate goodwill for the team before moving them from Boston to San Antonio. Which I..."

"Wait, what!" Kaylee said, her voice raising, slightly outraged. "The Red Hawks have always been in Boston."

"Does that really surprise you after meeting Elton Mock? The man doesn't even own a residence near where the team plays its home games. He doesn't care about the team, it's just what billionaire's do. Plus, I heard Texas is giving him a massive tax break to have the team move there. Zero percent property tax for 10 years, plus a brand-new stadium, and other miscellaneous tax breaks both local and state. And businessmen do not play around with tax breaks."

"I admit that offer sounds compelling, but the Red Hawks have been at Boston staple for over a century. He can't just move the team!"

"From my contacts, he can and he will as soon as he has the leagues approval."

"Is he going to get the leagues approval? I mean they won't just accept it, will they?"

"I believe they will."

"What about the team manager, the players? Don't our opinions matter?"

"No, not really, he owns the team."

"What if I talk with the players or the team manager? We could argue it. What if I went directly to the league?" Kaylee mentioned, feeling quite confident that she had found the solution.

"I should remind you again, he is a billionaire," Mr. Oakley finalized with a convincing tone.

Kaylee looked disappointed, but what could she do, Mr. Oakley was right, Mr. Mock was the owner, she was the player, even if the man was a creep. It certainly was his right, but still it bothered her.

"What if... I talked to him", Kaylee asked.

"I'm sorry? After what you said he did to you?"

"Yeah. If I talk to him, maybe I can convince him not move the team. The Red Hawks have always been a staple in the area, and it would be a shame to see them leave." Kaylee was trying to convince herself this was a good idea but wasn't quite sure herself yet. But part of being a player is that you need to put on a show, and she was going to do exactly that.

"You think he's going to ask again about his.... special request, right?"

"I know. And I am not going to give him what he wants."

Mr. Oakley sighed, trying to remain silent but a deep longing to ask a question burdened him. Kaylee noticed this; she had always been good at reading emotions.

"Come on, ask away," Kaylee said in a soft tone.

Mr. Oakley sighed again, not too sure he wanted to ask, but looking at her face, he felt assured that she was ready for it. He gathered some confidence and asked in a calm voice.

"I really shouldn't be asking this since you don't know me like that, but I feel like I get you in a higher sense than a reporter. I just wanted to ask, for your sake really. If everything came down to zero options and the only way out was to give in to Mr. Mock's demands, would you do it?"

That was deep! Definitely not the question she was expecting. Didn't he want to know anything about how much she was being paid? If she had collected the signing bonus? If she would ever leave the suburbs and move into a fine mansion in the hills?

"Don't get me wrong, Ms. Dyer," Mr. Oakley continued. "That question is not for you to answer to me. It is for you to think about actually."

Kaylee was already reading Mr. Oakley to not only be a very complicated man, but a direct and honest person. She had met few people like him, and very few as direct as him. However, she had no answers for him. She had never thought of it like that, and she hoped dearly that it would never come down to that.

"I'll.... talk to Mr. Mock," Kaylee simply replied softly.

"Well, if you're sure," Mr. Oakley said uneasily, he felt quite unconvinced about the outcome of her plan.

Kaylee took a deep breath and nodded her head. "I can't promise anything, but I can at least try."

"Just be careful out there," Mr. Oakley said uneasily. "You seem like a very decent person. From all I've read about you, all I've seen, how you play, how you communicate with the people around you, I know that you just really want to play baseball. It's a given passion and it's not going anywhere, at least I hope it doesn't go anywhere. You're an attractive person, that is true. But there are a lot of attractive women everywhere, but you, you have something to offer. You have a zeal, a strength like non other. That is the goal for Mr. Mock. It's really not about your attractiveness, it's about what he can get from the legendary Kaylee Dyer. And he'll do anything to get it, because you are not like the others, you are practically gold to him."

Kaylee was almost tearing up, and she felt another surge of hope flowing through her body. She had been reminded that being attractive is ordinary, but she wasn't only attractive, she was attractive and valuable, she was gold.

"Thank you, truly, I really needed that," Kaylee responded.

Mr. Oakley took down some notes. "Well, I think that concludes our business then. Like I promised, I won't write anything about Mr. Mock personally, but if you can save Boston its team.... well, that's worth an article." Mr. Oakley then dug into his pocket and pulled out a business card. "My card, be sure to tell me how it goes."

"Thank you, Mr. Oakley, I'll keep you in mind", Kaylee said, grabbing the card.

"Please, call me Ed. Mr. Oakley is my father."

"Well thank you Ed... and call me Kaylee."

"Will do... Kaylee," Ed said shaking her hand before placing some money on the counter and getting up.

"If you don't mind me asking," Kaylee said, making Ed stop abruptly in his steps. "You just sat down for over thirty minutes to listen to a story that doesn't concern you, gave an Oscar worthy speech and paid for my meal which you did not even taste. What's your deal? This doesn't seem like a regular reporter chase."

Ed smiled at Kaylee. "I'm just a reporter ma'am." And with that, he turned and left.

Kaylee held her breath until the reporter left the restaurant. What has she gotten herself into? She pulled out Mr. Mock's card and kept staring at the number on it. She contemplated hard if it was worth it to go to his house again, even the day right after her incident with him. But this was too important, she had to stop this which ever way she could. She felt convinced that he would listen to her. Wait, would he listen to her? And without asking for her?

Kaylee felt hopeless and angry at the same time. Remembering everything that happened the day before, she could barely hold back an outburst. No! She wasn't going to go to his house. She would find another way to solve this. Whatever it took, but not going to his house. There had to be another way, right?

———◉———

THERE WASN'T ANOTHER way.

Later that afternoon, Kaylee made her way back to Mr. Mock's home. She had called earlier to announce her coming, and Mr. Mock had sent her a limo again to bring her over.

Unlike yesterday, the limo ride was filled with apprehension. She didn't know if she could actually talk Mr. Mock out of moving the team, or worse. But still, it was something she had to at least try to do.

When the limo finally pulled up to the front entrance, the door was already open, and waiting for her, was Mr. Mock himself.

"Ah Kaylee, it's so good to see you again. I'm glad you've reconsidered." The way Mr. Mock said this made Kaylee squirm a little inside and was just plain unnerving.

"Of course, Mr. Mock. I want to play baseball. I would hate to see my career end over something that is not my fault."

Mr. Mock laughed at this. "On another note, there was something you mentioned that you wanted to talk about?"

"Uhh, yes, but can we do that inside."

"Of course we can", Mr. Mock said enthusiastically.

Kaylee felt ill as she remembered the day before. How could a human be so twisted?

Mr. Mock lead her to a small sitting room and sat down, and motioned for her to take a seat across from him. "So what did you want to talk about?"

Kaylee took a deep breath. This was the moment. There was no turning back now. "You're moving the team", she stated.

Mr. Mock's smile faded and was replaced with a stern expression. "Where did you hear about that?"

"So, it's true?" Kaylee asked.

"I never said that, nor denied it."

"Ok then, well whether if it is true or not, I think you should reconsider. Boston has a large fan base, and has always had the team, and the team has always had a following, a loyal one at that, for over a century. I think that moving the team would be a huge mistake."

Mr. Mock looked thoughtful, and tapped his finger against the chair. "Your thoughts are noted."

"I'm serious. The people would be devastated if we left. The Red Hawks have been around forever, and people want them to stay. I decided to be a baseball player because of that team."

Mr. Mock smiled. "Perhaps you are right. Perhaps I should reconsider. I mean, it would be a shame if a story came out, saying how the team was being moved, and all of the wonderful incentives that the state was giving us to make it happen."

Kaylee sighed, relieved. "Well, that's great then. Now, if you'll excuse me, I'll be leaving now."

"What?"

"I'd like to take my leave. I came to speak my heart to you, I did that. Now I must go."

"What the hell am I gonna do with your heart?"

"I don't understand."

"I thought you came here because you reconsidered my offer."

"Mr. Mock, I'm sorry if I gave you the wrong idea, but I'm not giving you my body to stay on your team."

"So, the team isn't worth it then, huh? Your life, your career, everything you've worked for since you were a little girl, you're just gonna throw all that away?"

"Are you really doing this right now? There are tons of beautiful women outside, ones that will die to have sex with you. Why are you so insistent on me?"

"Because you my dear are no ordinary woman, You're Kaylee Dyer, the first major league baseball player which I made happen by the way. You're a star with a beautiful face and a great ass, and that is what people like me want. I've worked too damn hard to be fucking cheap whores."

Kaylee Immediately rises to her feet with rage in her. "I am not giving you my body, and you're not going to be make me feel like a bad person for not doing so."

Kaylee turns to leave.

"You know, it's a shame you weren't able to mesh with the team and had to leave."

Kaylee paused in her tracks. "I'm sorry?"

"It's a shame the team won't work with you, and I have no choice but to fire you. It's a real shame, and I'll have to make a statement to the press."

"What are you talking about? Daryl is the only one who ever had a problem with me!"

"Oh, I seriously doubt that", Mr. Mock said, his expression unchanging. "My conversation with him was rather... enlightening, and my conversation with you when you broke into my home and tried to..."

"Broke in?", Kaylee said admonished. "You invited me here!"

"You have no proof of that. Mr. Adams and Mr. Jefferson will escort you off my property to an awaiting taxi, be glad I'm not calling the cops."

With that the two burly men who had escorted Daryl last time came back into the room and stood behind Kaylee.

"I hope you enjoyed your brief time as a professional player. The taxi will take you back to your hotel since it's already paid for. Once spring training is over though.... you're on your own."

With that Mr. Mock dismissed her, and she was escorted out. Once outside, she was shoved into the cab, and the two men slammed the door shut and waved her off.

She didn't say anything as the taxi took her back to her hotel, and once inside she was numb. It was over, her dream was over. She had been blackballed, and the only job she would probably get would be working in a bar or something, and that was only if she was lucky. Her career was over, her life was over. All because of Elton Mock.

Chapter 4
Depression

Kaylee had no idea what she was going to do now. She had only been playing professional league baseball for barely a week, and she was already fired. Worst of all, it over a matter that was completely not her fault. She felt that life really shouldn't be this hard, especially not to good people. All she wanted to do was play baseball, but now she had lost her chance and was now sunk in a lot of drama. There was also the fact that she was soon going to go broke.

Yet the only thing Kaylee seemed to be able to do was sulk and drink, in her already paid for hotel room. Baseball was everything to her, it was her life, and she was fired from it, and most likely blacklisted as well.

After drinking her 5th beer, Kaylee found herself crying again, and this time she had no Mel, or Little John to comfort her.

There was a knock at the door. Kaylee didn't bother to answer and get it. There was another knock. Kaylee ignored it. The knocking had finally stop, the unexpected guest had given up. She laid back for a long moment staring at the glass and silver chandelier wishing that her life could only work out as she had always fantasized it in her small house in the suburbs.

Suddenly, the sound of the door opening caught her attention. She turned around to find Ed Oakley standing there.

"How did you get in?", Kaylee slurred, having a little bit too much to drink.

"You have no idea how difficult it is to bribe a hotel receptionist", Mr. Oakley replied.

Kaylee didn't reply, instead opting to take another swig of beer. "This is all your fault, you know?"

Ed raised an eyebrow at this. "I'm sorry?"

"If you hadn't shown up, and told me about what Mr. Mock was planning, none of this would have happened!"

"I'm pretty sure based on what you told me, he was planing on doing so after you refused his advances. Besides, I'm a reporter, we report news."

Kaylee was silent, and then began crying again. "I don't know what to do."

"Well, first off, why don't we stop the drinking. Alcohol can't solve your problems."

"It can help drown them."

"Not really, it just drowns you for a moment", Ed replied, he didn't look impressed. "Look, I know it sucks, but if you're going to wallow in self-pity, you can at least do it while sober."

"And what fun is that? Then I'm just depressed with nothing to distract me. At least being drunk I can disguise my pain."

"No you can't. Trust me, I've been there."

"Well, that's easy for you to say. You still have a job and a career. I now have nothing and in a few weeks, I will be homeless."

Ed closed the door and walked into the room right in front of Kaylee.

"Listen to me. You can get through this, and you're not alone. I can help you. But you need to sober up and start thinking. O.K.?"

Kaylee stared at the reporter, and for the first time really got a good look at him. "Why are you helping me?"

Ed shrugged his shoulders. "It's the right thing to do, plus you're not the only one Elton Mock has screwed over before."

"How did he get you", Kaylee asked.

Ed laughed at this. "He didn't, but he tried to. It would seem a couple of years ago, one of his companies was in need of investors, and I had some money to invest. Well, after putting in the money, and the company making me a decent return, the company suddenly went bankrupt, and the owners were arrested for money laundering, that is except Mr. Mock. He made off like a bandit, having made a nice profit. No one could prove it, but they think the money laundering was his doing."

"I see, and why are you here?"

"Because, like I said, you're not the first, and I don't think you'll be the last. So, I'm going to expose him, and I need your help."

"And what's in it for me exactly?"

"I'm going to be honest, just full on revenge. That and a large enough scandal, and the ML will force him to sell, and you've already proven your actual talent. That was his mistake."

"So how are you going to prove anything?"

Ed chuckled. "Please, I'm a reporter. I'm going to expose the truth. All I need is to do some digging. But for that, I need you to pull yourself together."

Kaylee thought for a moment, and stared at Ed. She never noticed how red the man's hair was, and it seemed all to familiar, but she wasn't sure why. She felt truly convinced that this was the right thing to do, not just for herself, but for other people that Mr. Mock was probably going to ruin in the future.

"Nah, I'm good", Kaylee said, downing another large gulp of the beer in her hand.

"Come on Kaylee. This is going to be good for the both of us. You want to keep on playing baseball right?"

"Damn right I do."

"Show the world that you weren't fired because you're bad player."

"I'm not a bad player. I'm one of the best."

"I know, I didn't mean it like that", Ed rubbed his face with his palms. "We can prove to the world that Mr. Elton, quite contrary to what everyone else thinks, isn't a good man. He gets forced to sell and probably goes to jail somewhere in Russia, you get a good recognition, the team you've always wanted to play for calls you back since they already you're one of the best, and I get a story to report. Come on, what'd you say?"

Kaylee things on it again. This time more convinced and seeing reason in his words.

"Fuck it, I'm in."

"Great" Ed said clapping his hands together. "First things first however, you need to sleep off this alcohol."

Kaylee laughed at this.

Ed rolled his eyes. "All right, let's get you into bed. We'll talk about it more tomorrow."

Kaylee giggled. "Are you trying to take advantage of me?"

Ed looked horrified at this. "Go to sleep Kaylee."

"Okky dokkie", Kaylee said before collapsing on top of the bed. Ed sighed and looked at the messed up room, thinking he needed to clean it up for when Kaylee woke up.

———◉———

THE NEXT MORNING KAYLEE woke up and found the room was surprisingly clean. The only indication of her drinking was that the trash can was filled with empty beer bottles. She rubbed her forehead and felt a hangover headache coming on.

"Good you're up", a voice said.

Kaylee turned and found Ed sitting on the couch, watching her.

"Oh God, did we..." Kaylee stammered.

Ed laughed. "No. That I wouldn't do that. Do you remember what we talked about?"

"What we talked about?" Kaylee repeated, trying to remember.

"Yes, about Mr. Mock and baseball. Don't you remember?

"I do, but it was the night before. My memory is a little fuzzy."

Ed chuckled at this. "That tends to happen after drinking six beers in a row."

"Ha ha, very funny", Kaylee said, finally getting out of bed, "So now what?"

"Now we plan", Ed replied.

"Didn't we already do that?" Kaylee asked confused.

"That was the plan for the plan. Now we do the actual planning for the plan."

"Right, so what's the plan exactly."

"Well, first we're going to need witnesses. I doubt you're the only one on the Red Hawks who have beef with the guy."

Kaylee nodded in agreement.

"All right, so I'm going to need you to contact your teammates, and have them come to meet us."

"And if they ask why, I'll just say I want us to go out and do something as a group."

"Maybe", Ed shrugged. "I don't know, you know them best."

"Isn't it your job to know us?" Kaylee replied.

"Hmm, well yes, but I don't really know the team members personally, just their records, and what's public knowledge. Like your record, your history, and that you can't handle your liquor." Kaylee rolled her eyes at this.

"All right, let's start contacting the guys."

Chapter 5
Origins

23 Years Earlier
"Kaylee are you ready?" Her grandfather Peter called out. The piper-pater of small feet could be heard as a 5-year-old girl ran down the stairs and jumped into the older man's arms.

"Grandpa, grandpa, grandpa", the little girl said in excitement.

"Oh, ho, ho! How's my little champ?" Her grandfather said as he picked little Kaylee up in a twirl and taping her on the nose.

"Grandpa!" Kaylee once again said in excitement, giving a childish blush.

"Oh, sorry champ, I forgot you don't like that. But none of your friends saw, so that has to be worth something right?"

Kaylee giggled at this and hugged her grandfather rather enthusiastically, saying nothing else.

"Ready for our big day?" Her Grandfather asked.

"Yes", Kaylee said excitedly.

"Well then, let's get a move on then", her grandfather said, putting her down and grabbing her to walk her out of the house. Her parents watched on, as she entered her grandfather's car and began to drive away.

"So where are we going?" Kaylee asked from the backseat.

"I know you're a bit young, but have you heard of baseball before?"

Kaylee had heard the term before, but had never seen or played a game. She decided it would be best to answer no, and shook her head from the backseat indicating so.

"Well after today, you won't be able to say that anymore. I'm taking you to the Red Hawks vs New York game."

A large smile came onto Kaylee's face as she yelled out in excitement. She was glad to do anything with her grandfather, even doing something she had never done before and completely did not understand. A little while later, they pulled into the parking lot of the baseball stadium and got out, and went to search for their seats.

As it was a weekday, and the Red Hawks were not exactly known for their record, the stadium wasn't very full. This did not bother Kaylee, in fact, it made her happy because it meant less people. The Red Hawks however still had their loyal fans who would always show up for a game.

Kaylee was given a small bag of peanuts, which she ate happily, and a bottle of water, and then her grandfather explained to her what a baseball was and what it was used for, slowly, without knowing, he was explaining the complete intricasis of the game, the players, their positions, the teams, and even the MLB rooster. Little Kaylee found herself mesmerized by the tale, and just wanted to know more, but these thoughts were interrupted when a song was played, indicating the beginning of the game.

Kaylee found herself amazed as she watched the pitcher throw the ball. She had no idea why, but for some reason, she had an interest in the man who threw the ball.

She was not the only one that noticed, her grandfather saw this as well.

"Would you like to be a baseball player when you grow up, champ?" Her grandfather asked.

"Can I?" She asked, a little shocked. She had been watching attentively the whole time and even though she was a little girl, she had noticed clearly that there were no females on the field.

Her grandfather laughed at this. "Put your mind to anything, and you can achieve it."

Little Kaylee smiled at this and nodded her head, and returned to watching the game.

Later on, when the game was over, the Red Hawks had lost 3-2, but Kaylee had no cares. She was hooked and would never be able to let go.

The entire drive back home, her grandfather listened to her rattle off everything she loved about baseball. She loved the pitcher, the game, the way it was played, and how the fans acted. Being an aficionado of the sport, he was more than happy to listen, but knew her parents might think otherwise.

<hr />

FOR THE NEXT FEW DAYS, the only thing Kaylee could talk about was baseball. To her family, to her teachers, and even her best friend Caroline. Caroline was Kaylee's best friend since childhood. She was short and less attractive than Kaylee but was book smart and bolder than Kaylee. Sometimes, she would chase away lunch time bullies who tried to pick on Kaylee.

Caroline, was not a fan of baseball, and found the whole thing boring. Kaylee found this unacceptable, and took it upon herself to try and teach her friend the intricacies of the sport, much to her friend's dismay.

"So you see, to win a game, the two teams compete to score the most runs, one run at a time. Each player, except the pitcher, who begins the play as the batter's teammate, is required to run a series of four bases, starting from first base, continuing onto second base..."

"Yes, you've already told me this Kaylee!" Her friend snapped, showing far more annoyance than a typical 5 year old would show.

"Yes, but...."

Caroline put her hand up. "Let me stop you right there, I'm not a fan of baseball. You should know this. In fact, the only reason I'm here is because you said you had some cool toys." Kaylee looked hurt at this and was starting to cry.

"Fine", she sniffled, "follow me."

Caroline followed her friend to her bedroom and watched as Kaylee rummaged around until she found what she was looking for.

"Here", she said, handing a small red and white ball to her friend.

"Uhh, thanks?" Caroline said, looking unsure.

"You're welcome."

"Soooo, why did you give me this exactly."

"It's a baseball!"

"And?"

"It's an amazing sport!"

"Did you not listen at all to what I just said?" Caroline demanded.

Kaylee looked disappointed at this. "I did", she replied, looking hurt.

Caroline looked at the toy. "What is it even good for?"

"To play catch, and it can be used to hit, or to play stick ball. I've been reading up on everything you can do with one, asking as many questions as I can."

"O.K., I'll admit that sounds kind of fun, but why does the ball have to look like this."

"Like what", Kaylee asked, confused.

"The colors and the stitching."

"Hmm, I don't know. I'll have to add it to my list."

Caroline raised an eyebrow at this. "List?"

"Of things I need to learn about baseball, and why everything is the way it is. So far I've written down 23 questions."

"You're weird."

"I am not."

"You are, and so is your obsession with this sport."

"It's not an obsession. Baseball is amazing, and it's not just a sport", Kaylee said trying to defend herself.

Caroline stared at her friend for a few moments, but quickly saw she was losing the conversation. "Fine" she conceded.

"Want to go outside and play catch with me?"

Caroline rolled her eyes at this. "All right."

Kaylee smiled and took the baseball from her friend, and they both ran out the backdoor and into the yard.

BY TIME SHE WAS SEVEN, Kaylee's parent's had expected her obsession with Baseball to be a fad but couldn't be proven to be more wrong. In reality, her obsession only grew, and she began to demand to play little league, yet they refused. They had a view that this was not a sport for women, yet she persisted, and eventually they gave in, and signed her up for T-ball.

Though not entirely happy with the league chosen, Kaylee put her all into it, and soon surpassed everyone's expectations. At the coach's pleading, her parents eventually gave in and signed her up for proper little league.

At her first game, the opposing team refused to pitch to her, and she found this incredibly frustrating, as she was the best player on the team, she was sure of it. Still several outright refused to play so as to avoid getting cooties, to the post. Where the other team who cede the game. This certainly did not make her popular with the rest of her team, who like her actually wanted to play baseball.

This would continue on until one day her team, the Red River Dogs, were playing a team from out of town named the Blue Jackets. To her great surprise, they had no trouble playing with her, and for the first time in a while, she got to hit in a game. Kaylee was on her second at bat, and the score was 1-0 in favor of the blue jackets.

"Batter up, batter up," the catcher called.

Kaylee took a deep breath and prepared for the pitch.

"Ball," the umpire called.

Kaylee sighed, and the pitcher winded up for the next pitch.

"Ball two," the umpire called again.

The pitcher looked annoyed and threw the ball.

"Ball three," the umpire said once again.

Kaylee was getting angry now, and was starting to think this was on purpose. She didn't like this.

"Strike" the umpire suddenly called.

This caught her off guard, and she didn't swing.

"Strike two" the umpire said, catching her completely off guard.

"Come on kid, swing the damn bat!" the catcher yelled.

The pitcher grinned and wound up the ball.

Kaylee took a deep breath as the pitcher let the ball fly. Everything was moving fast now, but the sound of her bat connecting with the ball was unmistakable. She watched the ball fly and soar over the center field fence.

"Home run", the umpire said, and the crowd went wild. Kaylee began to run the bases, whilst the opposing team could only stand there and watch. When she had finally completed her laps, she was greeted by the rest of the team, cheering and praising her.

"Way to go kid, that was an awesome hit," the coach said with a big smile on his face.

"Thanks coach," Kaylee replied with a grin.

"Yeah, you really showed those jerks," their catcher said.

Kaylee smiled at this. "Thank you but for now, we have a game to win."

The game continued and the Red River Dogs came out victorious with 8-3 in their favor. Little did anyone know that inside Kaylee, finally being able to play the sport she loved for real, had ignited a fire. She was hooked, and never wanted to let go.

———◆———

KAYLEE CONTINUED TO play Little League, rising up through the divisions fast, and by the time she had gotten to high school, she had her parents full support for her passion. However, when she went to tryout for her High School team, she ran into a major setback.

"I'm sorry Ms. Dyer, but the school rules state that only boys can try out for the baseball team. If you want to play, you have to sign up for the girls softball team." The coach said this nonchalantly, seeming to not care if it hurt Kaylee or not.

"But that's a very different sport from Baseball!" Kaylee cried out.

"I'm not sure I follow. They seem pretty similar to me."

A look of horror was on Kaylee's face at this statement, and she began to ramble about the differences between the two sports. The coach held up his hand to stop her.

"Don't call our rules dumb, rules are there for a reason. And they'll stay that way even if you don't like them. Besides, I don't make those rules," the coach had spat out after having enough of Kaylee's shenanigans.

"It's not like you'd change them if you had the chance," Kaylee said shyly, hoping that she did not offend him. She did.

"I'm sorry, but those are the rules, and if you don't like them, talk to the principal."

Kaylee felt defeated, but still didn't like this. She actually marched off to the principal's office to demand an exception, but still found herself denied. "This calls for far more drastic measures" Kaylee thought to herself.

The next week, the baseball coach was surprised to find himself being pulled into the principles office where Kaylee Dyer, her parents, and a lawyer sat waiting.

"Mr. Harkness", the principle said, "please have a seat."

"Uhh, what is this about?" the coach asked, rather concerned.

"Why don't you have a seat, and we'll tell you."

The coach sat down in the only empty seat, which was in front of a table where the rest were seated.

"This is a lawsuit, brought forth on behalf of Kaylee Dyer for discriminating against her for her gender."

"I'm sorry?" the coach said exasperated.

"Ms. Dyer here has been playing since the age of 7. Now, you refuse to let her try out for the baseball team because of the rules you made. Rules that aren't district policy," the lawyer clarified on the lawsuit.

The principle and coach both looked nervous.

"She can play softball like the rest of the girls, or join the girls volleyball team."

Kaylee scoffed at this. "I want to play baseball, not softball."

The coach shrugged his shoulders. "Then go join another school."

Kaylee was fuming, as were her parents, and the lawyer looked stunned.

"Sir, you should be careful with what you are saying...." The lawyer began.

"I said what I said and I stand by it." The coach interrupted.

Kaylee, her parents, and their lawyer all stood up.

"It is clear we won't be able to come to an agreement. Have a nice day sirs." With that the family and lawyer left.

—————◆—————

"WHAT DO YOU MEAN THERE'S nothing we can do!" Kaylee exclaimed.

"I mean legally, the school has the right to not allow you on the team. There is nothing we can do legally."

"So I just give up?" Kaylee said, partially sulking.

"Oh I only said legally. You have other options."

"Like what?"

"Well if you remember, they did say to find a different school to play at. There is one, not too far away that does allow female students on their baseball team.

"That's over an hour's drive though!" Kaylee complained.

"Yes, but they have the rule you are looking for. It's your choice however."

Kaylee looked at her parents. By now, they fully supported their daughter in her ambition, and new she would go somewhere with it.

"So you'll really take me to the other school. You'd do that for me?"

"If it's what you really want sweetie, we'll do our best to support you."

Kaylee jumped up and down excitedly and hugged her parents, who laughed.

"I guess I'm going to be playing baseball at a new school," Kaylee said with a huge smile on her face.

"I'm sure you will do great dear" her mother said.

"Thanks mom," Kaylee said.

—————◆—————

KAYLEE'S GRAND-SLAM

KAYLEE'S NEW SCHOOL was a private one, and was incredibly receptive to her story, and after seeing her play, gladly let her onto the team. However, she did have to deal with the fact that there were no girls' bathrooms in the locker rooms, which was incredibly awkward.

Still, she was now on a team, and that is what mattered. Not only that, but it had to be fate that their first game was against her old school. She could hardly wait, and had the opportunity to show them just how much she had improved.

At the game, her parents were sitting in the stands, cheering her on.

"Good luck honey" her mother said.

"Thanks, mom", Kaylee said before putting on her helmet.

The game began and she was a bundle of nerves. When it was her turn at bat, her whole body was shaking.

"Calm down, deep breaths, relax", she told herself.

"Hey, girlie, are you going to bat or what" the catcher called out.

"Girlie?" she repeated quietly, getting annoyed. She tried to brush it off and took her position, and waited for the pitcher to throw the ball.

The pitcher took his position, and when he was ready, mounted up all his strength and threw the ball as hard as he could. Kaylee was unrelaxed, but also vexed. She swung the bat with all her might, giving it her every energy and focus. A loud crack was heard as it made contact with her bat, and before she even saw where it was going, Kaylee began running fast.

"Safe," the umpire called.

As she looked out into the crowd, she could see her parents smiling and cheering. This would repeat several times throughout the game, and it was becoming clear to everyone that Kaylee had something special about her.

The game wasn't even close, and was frankly embarrassing the other team. The best part was she got to watch the old coach look far away in shock at what he missed out on. Kaylee would continue to have repeated performances through the rest of the season and high school, and eventually settled on playing pitcher. Although they lost some games, it was always close.

By her Senior year, Kaylee knew she wanted to go professional. She was going to go professional no matter what.

Chapter 6
The Plan

Caroline Markham hadn't heard much from her best friend Kaylee Dyer since high school, which was not surprising considering they had gone to different universities and the woman had been signed to the MLB. They had been a tight string when they were little and went through high school.

Kaylee had always been the hot attractive one who got a lot of favors from the hot boys who had access to the big parties and the great events of high school. Caroline was the cute, not very attractive young lady who had the brains and blew everyone mind with her smartness and top grades. Caroline, unlike most other ladies her kind, wasn't a nerd, she was social, simple and idealistic, and still managed to be appealing to everyone else. Both Caroline and Kaylee had lots of differences and got on each others' nerves sometimes, but they never separated or stayed angry at each other for long, not when if their parents had something to say. They had only separated when they both discovered their paths and went their individual routes towards college. Caroline had always known of Kaylee's high interest in baseball and even though she always had her reservations about it, she knew that there was no stopping her friend and she had to give her her undying support.

She had always supported Kaylee all the way and hoped that she would achieve her then impossible dream of being the first female, major league baseball player. So, imagine her surges to find out she had quit her dream team after only one practice game. That honestly didn't sound like Kaylee at all, and there had to be something more to it.

Caroline really wanted to look more into it, but her job at the SEC tended to prevent it. However when she got a random text from Kaylee one night to meet up, she found herself unable to say no. She immediately got on a plane and headed straight for Florida where she would finally meet with her long time best friend. She wasn't too sure if they were still best friends, or if Kaylee had found another best friend. It had been such a long time of minimal communication between the two. However, her best friend, presumably, needed her and she had help if she can.

The bar Caroline arrived at was not her kind of scene, but she found her old friend easily enough. Kaylee hadn't changed much. She still looked like the hot young lady Caroline had always known, who stole all the attention and shared it with her. It was one thing she loved about her best friend, no matter what her attractive nature got her, she always remained humbled and would never leave her best friend hanging even for the hottest boys.

"There you are," Kaylee said excitedly.

"Hello, Kay," Caroline replied, unsure why she was here.

"Have a seat, I ordered us some drinks."

Caroline took her seat and looked at the drink in front of her.

"Beer", Caroline asked, not impressed.

"I can't get you wine and chocolate can I?"

Caroline smirked at this. "Ah.... are you sure?" she asked playfully, fluttering her eyelashes.

"Shut up", Kaylee said, equally as playful.

"So what's up, Kaylee, why did you ask me to come all the way down here?"

"Come on, can't I catch up with an old friend?"

"Old friend!"

"My old best friend"

"You didn't call me out all the way to this city to catch up, did you?" Caroline said with a smirk.

"You're acting like you don't miss me. I know you do," Kaylee replied with a shy grin as she seeped her beer.

"Fine, I missed you, a little bit. Now what was the very serious issue for which you call me here?"

"Oh, yes, that. Well, I was fired from my team, and I'm trying to make things right."

"Fired? The press conference said you quit!"

Kaylee rolled her eyes. "Of course he said that."

"Of course who said what?"

"The team owner. Some smug bastard."

"So I take it it's not true?"

"Nope. He's also a creep, and fired me because I wouldn't sleep with him."

Caroline choked on her drink.

"What?" she said, still coughing. "You can't be serious. Isn't he like a millionaire, aren't they surrounded by lots of free girls. Or is rich people getting free girls just not a thing anymore?"

"Well apparently he wants to sleep with women who have value. I'm sure you can relate to that."

"Uh, thanks for that statement first of all, but second of all, I cannot in fact, relate. But did he actually say it though? Like did he actually ask you to sleep with him?"

"Yeah, I didn't have a choice. Well technically he didn't say it out loud, but you can read between the lines."

"Well, if he didn't actually say anything...." Caroline started.

Kaylee raised an eyebrow at this. "What are you getting at?"

"Well do you have any proof. A recording maybe. Even voice will do."

"I don't have any of that. I didn't go to his house thinking he'd actually try anything like that. But you believe me right?"

"Of course I believe you. I'm just saying..."

"That it's not enough to build a case or anything I know. That's why I'm not building a case. Not yet at least."

"Well obviously what he did was abhorrent, but technically not illegal. But someone with that kind if personality isn't one to value the law as it is anyway."

"And?"

"Isn't it obvious? I have the ability to start inquiries to check for wrong doing. We do it all the time. Who is the owner by the way?" Caroline asked, genuinely curious.

"Elton Mock." Kaylee said, her bitterness towards the man evident.

"What the hell! That man is already on our shit list." Caroline said this rather gleefully, releazing it wouldn't take much to start an investigation into him.

"What's his deal?" Kaylee asked.

"Oh, the usual, tax fraud, embezzlement, money laundering\."

"That's the usual?"

"And those are just the charges we know of. Well that we know of, but haven't been able to prove. I might as well give it a shot, see if I have any better luck than my predecessors." Once she was in her investigative mode, Caroline could be scary.

"Can we really do this? I really need to bring this man down. Not even for me, but for everyone Elton Mock will want to do this too in the future. I might not even be the only person he's threatening right now." Kaylee said.

"Well we can do it legally by gathering a strong case against him. Cases to be on the safer side."

"And illegally?"

"I didn't say anything about that."

"But you were gonna say something about it right?"

"No, absolutely not."

"Well, good luck anyway."

"Thanks, I'll need it. What about you?"

"I might try to meet with some of the other players, and straighten some things out. Ask a few questions, see if they hate him as much as I do. Hopefully he's given them a reason to," Kaylee said genuinely.

"And how are you going to do that?" Caroline asked, a little skeptical.

"Oh, that's easy, I'll just call them. I still have all their numbers."

Caroline shook her head. "Of course you do."

"You think this is a bad idea?"

"No. Honestly, I'm happy you're doing something, and that I get to help."

Kaylee smiled at her friend. "Thanks and thank you for coming all the way here."

"No, problem, it's been too long since we hung out. We should do it more often."

"True that."

The two women laughed and did their best to enjoy the rest of their night, without further thought of Elton Mock in their heads. After a long while of laughter and giggling to gest from their past, they clinked their glasses of beer together and stayed silent for a long awkward moment.

"It's really nice to see you again, Caroline, truly," Kaylee finally said with a shy smile on her face.

"Yeah, yeah. It's nice to finally see you too," Caroline responded with a grin.

"You know, I always thought about you. All those years. It was kinda lonely if I'm being honest. A lot of the time I wished you were there, you know..."

"You really don't have to do all this, Kaylee. We're totally cool. I have nothing against you," Caroline interrupted.

"I know, I know. I just feel guilty a lot. You know I just deeped myself in my thing, I didn't really show support for your own thing. I wanted to play baseball soo bad I was willing to loose anything else for it. Even you. And I realize now, that I was wrong. And I'm sorry."

"Not everything. You didn't loose your dignity. And for that, I respect you. And I understand why you didn't reach out this whole time. Everyone has to put their dreams above all else, even their best friends."

"It's not like that..."

"But it's the truth. We must all accept it. It's okay Kaylee, we're cool, really. And we'll bring down this bastard together, like old times."

Kaylee stayed quiet for a long while, absorbing the truths coming from her friend, even though, she wasn't sure how they'd go about it.

"Come my hotel tomorrow, I've got something to show you," Caroline added with a nervous gaze to the window outside. She refused to look at Kaylee as she spoke, which gave Kaylee a suspicious feel.

"What is it?" Kaylee asked, genuinely inquisitive. She felt that this wasn't good but didn't understand what it was either.

"Just come around, you'll find out. I promise, you'll like it."

Kaylee smiled, satisfied with her friends understanding. She raised another glass of beer in the air. "To old times."

Caroline smiled, then raised her own glass and clinks with Kaylee's. "To old times."

———⬦———

ED OAKLEY WAS SPENDING another late night at the office. Since his meeting with Kaylee, he had gotten a new found energy in the case against Elton Mock. He had been working on this for years, checking every nook and cranny, interviewing everyone he could get to, to find some form of information on Elton that he could release to the public to show that Elton Mock wasn't the likable personality that everyone thought he was. However, all he ever got was information, lots of it, but without proof. There was never any viable evidence he could use to ruin Elton's image. But now, meeting Kaylee, someone he had convinced to join him in his escapade, things would be different now and he could actually get ahead now. He had put in many late nights and tiring efforts of research in the office, but if everything went according to plan, it would be worth it. He was finally going to take down Elton Mock, he would finally get his just desserts.

This being a sports related issue made things all the better, and the editor was very interested to learn Kaylee had been fired, not quit. He already had another more formal interview with Kaylee coming up, and he just hoped her contacts with the team and SEC paid off. Information like this from the rest of the team and especially the team manager, if tallying with that of Kaylee's, could really take their scheme a long way ahead.

"What an odd combination of contacts to have", he thought to himself.

It was no matter, they had a story, and he would soon have the truth. He was sure that Elton must have had issues with some other team members. Or at least done something suspicious that one of the team had taken note of. The truth would set the world free.

The phone suddenly began to ring, and Ed grabbed the receiver. "Ed Oakley, Northeast Sports", he said, not caring who it was.

"You think you're a hot stuff, don't you?", the voice on the line said.

"I'm sorry?" Ed replied, not sure how to respond.

"You think you can bring me down. I've been here for years, I know the system. I know how this fucking world works.

I even know how you work. I can bring you down with a blink. You here me kid?"

"Who the hell is this and what the hell are you talking about?" Ed spat out with an angry outburst. He was starting to have enough of it.

"Don't act all coy. I'm talking about Kaylee Dyer. You're trying to get her back into the limelight, and expose me, aren't you."

Ed realized immediately who was speaking. "Mr. Mock I presume? I must say, anything that comes out is your own doing, I only report the facts."

"That is not how the world works kid!" Mr. Mock exclaimed, raising his voice.

"Then how does it work", Ed asked calmly.

"The way I saw it does! You see the rich, the powerful, you are none of those things. People like you don't win, they endure. You just take whatever we decide to give you and be fucking happy about it."

"Did you try to get her to sleep with you to maintain her spot on the team?"

Mr. Mock laughed hard at this. "You think you're gonna trap me on a recorded call, I'm not stupid Oakley. I've been in this game before you were born. I'm not stupid."

"I highly doubt that", Ed replied, still eager to get a confession out of him. "See you messed with the wrong person this time. Kaylee Dyer, isn't like any other woman you've ever met, she's smarter than you, she's stronger than you and unlike these other girls you mess around with, she has principles, and she's not gonna break them to work for you, Mock."

"What do you want, huh? Money? A promotion? You wanna be chief editor, one call and I'll make that happen."

"What are you scared? You didn't actually ask her to sleep with you, did you Mock?"

"Fuck you Oakley!"

Ed laughed quietly under his breath, he knew he had struck a nerve and was enjoying this.

"How's your father, Oakley?"

Ed's face suddenly sunk, he stood up from his seat and attempted pacing around but the phone line couldn't stretch further than his office. He grabbed the office phone and unplugged it from the power cable, then walked to the large window, overlooking a beautiful view of the city.

"Don't you dare!"

"What was it, mild shock that somehow led to a heart attack? Oh no, the man got soo depressed because he was loosing his mind, seeing that he couldn't amount to anything, couldn't provide for his family right? So he decided to take his own life, leaving behind a scared little boy and a woman who took care of toddlers for a living. Maybe he wasn't a man after all. Is that about right? Did I miss anything?"

Ed remained silent, recounting the events that led to his fathers death. Mr. Benet had sunk all the family had into an investment into a startup that had promised a very high rise with very little downsize risk, unfortunately, the startup surprisingly went bankrupt and Mr. Benet lost everything. Ed was only sixteen at the time but was old enough to understand what had happened. His father had suffered in depression for the rest of his life and no matter how much Ed's mother tried, his father just couldn't live with the fact that he had lost the house, the car and the family savings to the bankruptcy of a startup that projected high yields. Mr. Benet swallowed depression pills all the time and eventually overdosed on it. Ed only came back home from public school on a hot Friday afternoon to find his father lying down lifeless on the bathroom floor.

"Hello! Hello! Oakley are you there?" Elton Mock yelled out through the phone.

"You have no idea what my mother and I went through", Ed replied as tears filled his eyes. "I had to walk from school everyday. I would wake up and have to pray that God provides something for my mother and I to eat. I sold sunglasses to tourist on the weekend to get through school. All because you..."

"Oh shut up with all that. You have no proof of all this. Whatever happened to you happened because that is what you deserve, that is what the universe decided to give you. Don't blame it on me. I'm just a billionaire trying to live a good life."

"I will come for you, I will get you so hard..."

"You will not get shit! You listen to me, you better drop this nonsense or you can better well expect me. I will come at you with everything I've got. And trust me, you don't want to go against me."

"You won't believe how much I want to."

Elton chuckled then took a deep satisfying sigh. "Listen kid, you're not one of us. We're the rich, the powerful, we decide how things go and you, you just sit down and do what we tell you to do. You will never be one of the big dogs kid."

"Well, as it turns out, neither will you be in just a little bit." Without saying another word, Ed hung up. He was soo angry he attempted to fling the phone out the window but a voice from behind held him back.

"Sir!", said the office Janitor. "Are you okay sir?"

Ed turned around, realizing that he was about to destroy office property. He took a deep sigh and wiped his face.

"I'm fine, thank you."

"You don't look okay. It actually looks like you were about to throw the office phone out an open window. People park down there you know. Do you need a handkerchief or something?"

"I'm good, really. Thank you."

Looking at the clock, he decided it was enough for the night, packed up, and headed out. He was glad the next day was Saturday.

———◦———

KAYLEE SAT DOWN ON her bed and pulled out her phone. She was going to do the one thing she dreaded, reach out to her former teammates. She felt awkward, and hoped they would answer, or not ignore her. Really, she was just hoping that they would listen to her at all.

She took a deep breath. "Here goes nothing."

She started by sending a text to Mel and Little John. Though she trusted him, she was not going to involve the team manager in this at all.

After she was done texting, Kaylee fell back onto her bed. She knew they were her friends, her teammates, but couldn't be sure that they would even want to hear her out. She only had a few days left before she would be homeless, and stranded in another state.

She knew that the two men would understand her situation and what she had to do. She could only hope the rest of the team would understand, and maybe, just maybe, would be willing to fight Elton with her. God knows she could really use two muscular built men.

MEL HAD BEEN CONCERNED when their new teammate just quit out of the blue after only one practice game. No goodbyes, not even a press conference, just gone. He simply didn't understand why, especially given her performance in the game. He really hoped he hadn't discouraged her in his pep talk.

No, that couldn't be it. It must have had something to do with that meeting of hers with Mr. Mock. Daryl had returned fine, a bit wheel shocked and roughed up it seemed, but fine none the less. Kaylee simply just didn't come back.

In the back of his mind was a horrible thought. What if Mr. Mock had kidnapped Kaylee and was keeping her locked in his attic. No, no, that was a horrible thought, and couldn't happen. Right?

Suddenly his phone vibrated, indicating a text message. Very few had his number, he liked it that way, and they knew when to contact him. So if someone was texting him now, it had to be important. He pulled out his phone and checked the messages.

Kaylee: Hey guys, can you talk?

Little John: I can, can't speak for Mel.

Mel: I can talk.

Kaylee: I'm sorry, but I've got to explain myself. It is probably best to do so in person. Can you meet me tomorrow?

Mel: Sure.

Little John: Works for me.

Kaylee: Great, let's meet at 9. There's a coffee shop called Brews Brothers.

Mel: Weird name but it's cool.

Little John: See you then.

Mel smiled as he put his phone away. Well, at least she was safe. Suddenly a hint of concern came to his face. What is it she wanted to talk about? What ever it was, it can't be good if she wants to talk to them alone in person. Well, he'll find out soon enough. Soon, he would have his answers.

Chapter 7

The Set Up

B rews Brothers was a well known local restaurant that had seen great success, especially in the spring when the Red Hawks did their spring training, the restaurant would have fans flocking into it after a nice day of watching their favorite team train. But today at 9 AM, there was hardly anyone, a surprise to be sure, but a welcome one for three individuals that were meeting here. Especially if anyone ever realized who these individuals were.

Mel and Little John entered the restaurant and looked around. There were only a handful of other people in the building, but none of them seemed to fit the description of their former teammate.

"I don't see her", Little John said.

"Eh... we're early." Mel suggested. Little John shrugged at this, considering it plausible.

Wanting to be thorough however they both looked again, and almost wanted to smack themselves when they finally saw Kaylee sitting in a far corner of the restaurant. They both soon walked over to the table and greeted their one time teammate.

"Hi guys, thanks for coming", Kaylee said.

"Hey, Kaylee, long time no see", Little John replied.

"Yeah, sorry about that. I didn't really have a choice."

Both men looked confused at that, remembering what the team manager had told them about her departure.

"What do you mean by, 'not have a choice'? We were told you quit, just like that", Little John asked.

Kaylee took a sip of her drink and without missing a beat said what she was thinking out loud, "I was fired by Elton Mock, for not accepting Mr. Mock's sexual advances, and for digging to far into his scheme to have the team moved to San Antonio."

Both Mel and Little John's eyes widened at this revelation.

"Are you serious?", Mel asked, trying to remain calm.

"Yes."

"So, when you say you didn't have a choice...." Little John began,

"He's the owner, he can do whatever he wants, and he has a lot of influence."

"You could always sue him. Wrongful termination and sexual harassment?" Little John suggested.

"No, I already thought of that", Kaylee said, waving him off, "he's rich enough to make evidence disappear, not that I have any, anyway. Plus I tried something like that back in High School to get in the baseball team. It didn't work out and I ended having to go to another school so that I could play."

"Well.... shit", Mel said, shaking his head. Suddenly a thought came to him. A horrifying thought to him anyway. "What was that bit about him wanting to move the team?"

"Oh, well, he's moving the team to San Antonio, and wants a new stadium built for him. The stadium he wants is 450 million dollars, which is way over the price of the existing one, which is in pretty good condition. They agreed to build it."

"By they you mean?"

"The state government. They're also giving him zero tax, and no business man refuses an offer with zero tax. He's moving the team as soon as he gets the league's approval."

Both men looked surprised at this, nor where they happy at this news. If she had to guess she'd guess neither of them wanted to move from New England to Texas.

"Well... shit", said little John, being far more exclaimed than normal. "I just bought a new house in Boston."

"Tell me about it", Mel said, clearly looking displeased at the news. "So Mr. Mock is a jackass. Not only a regular one, but a misogynist one who hides behind a mask. Perfect, just perfect. Aren't we in the perfect team."

Kaylee nodded. "He also may have committed several financial crimes, but that's not hear nor there, and doesn't concern you too much."

The two men looked confused at her, wondering how her finding the owner committing financial crimes did not concern them.

"I don't follow, and why did you call us?"

"Well, the SEC is investigating him now, and has a source who can get proof. But he's rich enough, I'm not sure anything will stick."

"True, true", Little John said.

"So now what?" Mel asked.

"Well, if you can tell the rest of the team what really happened... I'm closest to you two, I hope you don't mind that. As a result, I felt more comfortable telling you two than anyone else."

"Of course Kaylee", Mel said, giving her a knowing look. "I'll be sure to tell the entire team, what happened... even Daryl."

"Thank you", Kaylee said, holding back tears from the raw emotions.

"So now, what's gonna happen to you?"

"Well, figure out a way back to Boston and try to pick up my life from there. The thing is, I've nearly dedicated it all to baseball thus far."

"You mean he didn't even give you a way back!" Mel exclaimed admonished.

"Yup. I only had a place to stay because the hotel was already paid for."

Mel was shocked, but Little John was angry. Without saying a word further, he pulled out his wallet, took out a couple hundred dollars in cash, and put it right in front of Kaylee. He asked for nothing in return, and said nothing.

Kaylee looked in shocked. "Thank you." Little John continued to look on in silence.

"Well I guess that's it then, good luck wherever life takes you Kaylee. Don't worry about the bill, I'll take care of it." Mel said this in a tone that said there would be no negotiation.

Kaylee simply blinked in response, said thank you more time. She collected her things and left, leaving Mel and Little John alone.

They sat in silence for a few moments.

"Wow, just wow." Mel said, breaking the silence.

"Agreed."

"Why did you do that?"

"Why not. I have money. If she needed help, I could help. She's not a bad person, was a good teammate, and was our friend. What was the point of me keeping it, or just leaving her here?" Little John left it at that, and was suddenly deep in thought.

Mel considered this and agreed. "I guess we should head to practice."

"I guess."

"Boy will they be surprised to hear what actually happened."

"You think we should tell them before or after practice."

———◦———

THE TEAM HAD BEEN RATHER confused when they had been informed Kaylee had left, but when Mel told them what happened, it all made sense, and everyone was rather upset. Well, everyone, save for Daryl that is.

"We're better off without her", Daryl declared.

The rest of the team looked at him with a mix of horror and anger, towards their teammate. By this point they had had enough of the man and were ready to finally speak their minds.

"I don't think she was all that bad." One teammate said.

"I thought she was great!" Another declared.

"Daryl, just because she wouldn't sleep with you doesn't mean you can hate her", Mel told their troublesome comrade.

"I don't know what you are taking about" Daryl said in a voice that no one actually believed. "It's the principle of it, women should not play baseball."

"Shut the fuck up" Mark Wats yelled at Daryl. This surprised everyone as he was not one to use such vulgar language, especially when his reputation was that of the wholesome good boy of the team. On Daryl's part, he looked speechless, and without saying another word, simply got up and left the room.

Mark sighed. He had not meant to yell at him, and certainly didn't want to make things worse.

"I guess that settles it, were going to fight back, aren't we?" Mel asked.

"I'll be damned if I let this slide." Another teammate said.

"I thought the same", Little John said.

"Me too", Mark said.

"Let's do this then", Mel declared.

The rest of the team agreed and soon the locker room was full of energy and excitement. Soon enough, a plan began to form to defend Kaylee on their end. No one messed with the Red Hawks and their players, not even the owner. Elton Mock would regret his actions that day, that they knew for sure.

———⊚———

KAYLEE HAILED A TAXI, her heart pounding with anticipation as she climbed into the back seat. The ride to Caroline's hotel was a blur of city streets and towering skyscrapers, but Kaylee barely noticed as she marveled as the sights passing by.

Arriving at the hotel, Kaylee stepped out of the taxi and gazed up at the grand facade, admiring its elegant architecture and sparkling glass windows. She made her way through the revolving doors, greeted warmly by the doorman as she stepped into the luxurious lobby.

"Good morning, how may I help you ma'am?" the receptionist greeted.

"I'm here to see Ms. Caroline Markham," Kaylee replied.

"Oh, I'm sorry, I cannot give out customer information," the receptionist mentioned cautiously.

"Oh, I'm not asking, I know she's in room 212,"

"Oh, well if she's expecting you, then you can just go right ahead."

"Thank you," Kaylee finalized and began to walk towards the left. The receptionist immediately called her back.

"The elevator's that way," the receptionist said, flashing Kaylee a bright smile as she checked her into the elevator. Kaylee returned the smile, her excitement building with each passing moment as she walked the opposite way.

As the elevator ascended to the 11th floor, Kaylee's heart raced with anticipation. She couldn't wait to see Caroline again, to catch up and share stories of their lives, but she was absorbed in the thought of the surprise that Caroline had for her. Caroline wasn't even the type to give surprises, and she was always serious about everything. Even growing up, Caroline was not like the others, she saw a lot of things others did as a waste of time, it's no wonder she grew up to be so successful.

Stepping out onto the 11th floor, Kaylee followed the hallway to room 212, excitement bubbling in her chest. She reached the door and knocked eagerly, waiting for Caroline to answer. To her surprise, the door swung open to reveal an elderly couple stepping out of the adjacent room 213. Kaylee blinked in confusion, momentarily thrown off by their unexpected appearance.

"Excuse me," she muttered apologetically, sidestepping the couple as she entered Caroline's room.

"Kaylee, darling, it's so wonderful to see you!" Caroline exclaimed, pulling Kaylee into a warm hug.

"I mean we met a few days ago but likewise, Caroline," Kaylee replied, returning the hug with equal enthusiasm. "But why did you ask me to come? Is everything alright?"

Caroline's expression faltered for a moment, before she quickly plastered on a smile. "Oh, everything's just fine, dear. I simply wanted to catch up and spend some quality time together."

Kaylee sensed that Caroline was avoiding the real reason for her invitation, but she didn't push further. Instead, she joined Caroline at the table, eager to enjoy breakfast and conversation with her dear friend. But as they chatted and laughed, Kaylee couldn't shake the feeling that something was amiss. She couldn't understand why Caroline was being so evasive, and her curiosity only grew stronger with each passing moment.

"I really need to know why you called me though and what is the surprise you had for me?" Kaylee questioned again, growing more enthusiastic. Her voice was now tinged with seriousness and her face was squeezed with a frown.

"Come on Kaylee, we'll get to that. Let's just have a moment of our own."

"I do want us to have a moment of our own but you already told me that you have a surprise for me and now it's just messing with my head. Come on, tell me what it is."

"Just relax, Kaylee..." Caroline said again.

"Are you getting married?"

"What?"

"Cuz we said we were gonna get married together."

"Well first of all, that is just dumb, time of marriage is kinda the dudes choice and secondly, no, I am not getting married. If I was getting married you'd be the first to know."

"So no man?"

"Fuck no, there is a man. I'm not stupid..."

"Hey I don't have man," Kaylee spat back with a nervous look.

"Really, still? What about Kevin?"

"Kevin's an idiot. He doesn't want kids."

"Why would anyone not want kids?..."

"That is not the point," Kaylee interupted, finally tired of all the forwards and backwards. "Tell me what the surprise is."

"Well if you must know so bad, the surprise are on their way."

"Are? Is it people?"

"Something like that."

Kaylee laid back thinking for a while as Caroline sipped her coffee and watched her. She wondered who it would be, she knew for certain that she and Caroline weren't connected to many people during their school days. She tried hard to think of the few people whom she and Caroline knew that would also fly to Florida to see her. Suddenly her nervous face suddenly changed to frown.

"You didn't...!"

Suddenly, there was a knock at the door, interrupting their conversation. Caroline excused herself and went to answer it, leaving Kaylee alone with her thoughts. Caroline jumped to the doorway and accompanied in two familiar faces. Kaylee's heart skipped a beat as she realized who they were: her parents, standing awkwardly in the doorway with hesitant smiles on their faces.

"Kaylee, darling, look who's here!" Caroline exclaimed, gesturing for her parents to enter the room.

But instead of feeling overjoyed at the sight of her parents, Kaylee felt a surge of frustration and anger. She hadn't seen them in years, and now they were just showing up unannounced? And when she had finally made something of herself.

"Caroline, what is this?" Kaylee demanded, her voice tinged with annoyance. "I didn't come here to see them."

"Kaylee, come on, they're your parents," Caroline replied.

"I DON'T CARE! I don't care. I don't want to see them," Kaylee spat out.

Kaylee's mother, Mrs. Dyer tried to move closer to her, "Kaylee, please."

"Don't you dare touch me," Kaylee yelled out as she moved back. "I don't want to ever see you two again in my life."

"Kaylee," Mr. Dyer said. "It's been eight years, we miss you. We want to put everything behind and be a family again."

"You missed me?" Kaylee said, anger burning in her eyes. "You rejected me, when I needed you the most. You made me look like an idiot. I trusted you! I trusted you as my parents! You were the only ones I had and you betrayed me! I thought you loved me!"

"We do love you, darling," Mrs. Dyer jumped in. "We just did what we thought was best for you. It's really what any parent would do."

"I didn't want you to be any parents. I wanted you to be my parents."

Kaylee grabbed her purse off the bed then turned to leave. However, her father jumped in front of her and began to plead with her.

"Kaylee, listen to me, your mother and I are sorry. We have tried reaching out, we wrote letters, we called, we tried everything to find you. But everyone who even had an idea of where you were wouldn't even tell us cuz they said you didn't want to be found... well not by us. We are sorry, we know we did not do right to you but we want to fix that. Anything. Please, tell us anything you want us to do, we're ready to do it."

"Really, you'll do anything?"

"Anything Kaylee."

Kaylee leaned in closer for her parents to hear her perfectly. "Leave me alone."

Caroline was taken aback by Kaylee's reaction, she knew her parents had hurt her, but she didn't think that Kaylee would still be bitter after years of not seeing them. Kaylee turned to Caroline before walking out, "This was not a pleasant surprise."

Caroline's smile faltered, her eyes flickering with concern. "I thought it would be a nice surprise, dear. I didn't mean to upset you."

But Kaylee was already shaking her head, her patience wearing thin. "I'm sorry, Caroline, but I need some time alone. Please, just give me some space."

With that, Kaylee turned on her heel and stormed out of the room, leaving Caroline and her parents standing in awkward silence behind her. As she rode the elevator back down to the lobby, Kaylee couldn't shake the feeling of betrayal that gnawed at her heart. She needed time to process her emotions, to come to terms with the unexpected reunion with her parents. But one thing was for certain: she wouldn't let anyone dictate her feelings or force her into a situation she wasn't ready for.

Kaylee rushed out of the hotel lobby, her steps echoing in the quiet morning air. She didn't bother with pleasantries as she hurried past the valet stand, snatching the keys to her rented car without a second glance. With a quick jerk of the door handle, she slipped into the driver's seat and slammed the door shut. The engine roared to life as she peeled out of the parking lot, the tires screeching against the pavement.

As she drove, her mind raced with a whirlwind of emotions. Anger, betrayal, confusion – all tangled together in a messy knot inside her chest. She couldn't believe her parents had the audacity to show up after all these years, as if nothing had ever happened between them. The memory of their abandonment still stung, fresh and raw despite the passage of time. Tears blurred her vision as she sped down the highway, her foot pressing harder on the accelerator with each passing mile. She barely noticed the flashing lights in her rear view mirror until the sound of a siren pierced through her thoughts. Panic surged through her veins as she realized she was being pulled over by the police.

Kaylee's tears blurred her vision as she drove, her mind consumed by the unexpected encounter with her parents. Unaware of the police car trailing her, she didn't notice the bus full of children until it was too late. With a surge of panic, she slammed on the brakes and turned the driving wheel at the same time, but the car skidded out of control. It spun wildly, causing bystanders to gasp in horror. The screech of tires echoed through the street as the car veered dangerously close to the curb before finally coming to a stop.

As the dust settled, Kaylee's heart raced with adrenaline. She took a shaky breath, her hands trembling on the steering wheel. The realization of what could have happened sent chills down her spine. Panic surged through her veins as she realized she was being pulled over by the police. Her heart pounded as two officers approached her vehicle, their expressions stern as they rapped on the window with the butt of their flashlights.

"Ma'am, step out of the car with your hands raised," one commanded, his voice firm and authoritative.

Kaylee complied, her movements slow and unsteady as she stepped out onto the asphalt. She felt like cornered animal, trapped and vulnerable under the glare of their scrutiny. But even as they barked orders at her, she couldn't bring herself to care. All she wanted was to escape, to run away from the pain and confusion that threatened to consume her.

Ignoring their demands, Kaylee turned away and began to walk, her steps faltering as she stumbled over the uneven ground. The officers shouted after her, their voices growing more insistent with each passing moment. But Kaylee was lost in her own world, her thoughts consumed by memories of a past she couldn't change. She suddenly raised her head and turned to address the people and the cops.

"I am sorry," Kaylee said with tears flowing down her face, her sorrow was evident. "I didn't mean to hurt anyone. It's just been a really fucked up week. I guess a lot of you have seen me on television or somewhere, but I really have more problems than a sexual assault and playing baseball. I just really can't handle all of this right now. I'm sorry."

The officers and all the onlookers, giving her a good glance, understood that she was obviously under a terrible situation. They all watched her with pity as she took one slow step after another.

The crowd that had gathered around the scene watched in silence, some murmuring in disbelief at the near miss. Kaylee felt their eyes on her, their gazes heavy with concern and curiosity. She swallowed hard, trying to push down the lump in her throat as she scanned the faces around her. Despite the chaos and commotion, Kaylee's mind remained fixated on the encounter with her parents. The emotions stirred up by their unexpected appearance threatened to overwhelm her, but she pushed them aside for now, focusing instead on the present moment and the relief of escaping unscathed.

As she reached the entrance of her hotel, she pushed open the heavy glass doors and stepped inside, the cool air of the lobby washing over her like a soothing balm. People greeted her with smiles and nods as she passed by, but she barely registered their presence. Her mind was elsewhere, lost in a haze of pain and regret.

Taking the stairs two at a time, Kaylee made her way up to her room, her chest heaving with exertion as she reached the door. With a shaky hand, she fumbled for her key card and slid it into the lock, the mechanism clicking open with a soft whir.

Inside, the room was dim and quiet, the only sound the gentle hum of the air conditioner. Kaylee stumbled over to the bed and collapsed onto the mattress, her body wracked with sobs. Tears streamed down her cheeks as she curled into a ball, her heart heavy with the weight of her emotions.

For hours, she lay there in the darkness, lost in a sea of grief and despair. But gradually, as the minutes turned into hours, a sense of calm washed over her like a wave. The storm inside her began to subside, replaced by a quiet sense of acceptance. And as the first light of dawn crept through the curtains, Kaylee closed her eyes and let herself drift into a restless slumber.

Chapter 8
The Offer

Elton Mock, the imposing figurehead of the Red Hawks, paced the expanse of his study with an air of restless agitation. His normally composed demeanor was replaced by an undercurrent of anxiety that posed beneath the surface. Back and forth he strode, his footsteps echoing off the polished marble floors, a testament to the turmoil that churned within him.

"Why him of all people?" Elton mused to himself, his thoughts swirling in a vortex of confusion and frustration. He had always prided himself on his ability to control every aspect of his meticulously crafted empire, but now, faced with the specter of rebellion from within his own ranks, he found himself teetering on the edge of panic.

The notion that any of this could be his fault, that his own actions and decisions had led to this moment of crisis, was a thought too unbearable to entertain. In Elton's world, he was always right, always in control, and the idea of his worldview being fundamentally flawed was a concept that simply did not compute.

Instead, Elton cast about for someone-anyone-to shoulder the blame for the chaos that threatened to unravel his carefully constructed facade of power and authority. And in his mind, there were two individuals who bore the brunt of his wrath: Kaylee Dyer and Ed Oakley.

Kaylee, with her audacious defiance and unwavering determination to challenge the status quo, had become a thorn in Elton's side, a constant reminder of his own fallibility. And Ed, with his nose where it didn't belong, had unwittingly stumbled upon secrets that threatened to expose Elton's darkest truths.

In the depths of his despair, a twisted smile crept across Elton's lips as an idea began to take shape in his mind. Divide and conquer, he thought to himself, the age-old strategy of manipulation and deceit. It was a tactic as old as time itself, but in Elton's hands, it was a weapon of unparalleled potency.

———◉———

KAYLEE SAT QUIETLY on her hotel bed, watching the news, and listening to the reports of a scandal involving Elton Mock. The SEC had announced an investigation into some last transactions of Elton, and his only response was to call anyone who asked him about it sheeple. From what she could tell, he was legitimately loosing it, and several of his fans were beginning to turn their backs on him.

"Good", she thought.

Suddenly and without warning, she got a text from an unknown number.

"Hmm, well that can't be good", Kaylee thought to herself. She opened the message and saw the following words:

Hello Kaylee, this is Elton Mock, and I would like to speak with you. I have an offer for you, an offer that will allow you to return to your old life and be a member of the Red Hawks once again. Please meet me tomorrow morning at 9 AM, and please don't be late.

Kaylee blinked as she read the message several times, not sure what to make of it. Elton had a habit of not using contractions, but the tone of the message was not something she had expected. Now, she had a dilemma on her hands.

"Well fuck", Kaye said slowly. This was certainly a major wrench thrown into their plans. Is this not what she wanted, to play baseball? She could be back on the team! But there has to be a catch, there's always a catch. What could Elton Mock want?

Kaylee took a deep breath. Well, there was only one way to find out, and it was not like she could refuse. She wondered if there was a need to reply. No, she wouldn't act desperate, even if she was. She dreaded her current life and would do anything morally right to be back with her favorite team. But she couldn't afford to make it seem that she wanted this more than he did. She tossed the phone on the bed and laid back smiling to herself. She felt she was finally winning. On second thought, just to be on the safer side. She turned and grabbed her phone.

Kaylee: Sure, 9 AM it is.

Kaylee sent the text and hoped she would not regret it. She immediately decided then to call Ed, and see what he had to say.

The phone rang, and then was answered.

"Hello, Northeast Sports, Ed Oakley speaking, how may I help you?"

"Mr. Oakley, it's Kaylee Dyer."

"Oh, Ms. Dyer, thank you for getting back to me."

"What did you expect, I called you after all. I was calling about something important."

"Go ahead."

"I have an appointment with Elton Mock tomorrow."

"Oh, is that so. Why?"

"I was asked to meet him, and I'm going. He, is offering... me back a spot on the team."

There was silence. "I see", Ed said after awhile. "Are you going to accept?"

"I... I don't know. It's everything I wanted, but there has to be a catch, there is always a catch in these sorts of things."

"You're right there is, still I wouldn't blame you, however I think I know what is going on." Ed said this confidently, to the point that Kaylee was paying attention to see what he would say next with extreme prejudice.

"Oh, and what would that be" Kaylee asked.

"You were his pawn, and are still his pawn, and now he's using you to distract us."

"What makes you so sure." Kaylee was slightly insulted, but willing to hear him out.

"He wants to decide a conquer, as he sees several enemies working together against him. Me, you... and even the rest of your team."

"What do you mean?" Kaylee asked, genuinely confused.

"They announced a press conference on their own in a few days. Something big is going to happen, and this is scaring Mr.

Mock. If he can divide us, he can take us all down, but if he can't."

"I see", Kaylee said coldly. She couldn't believe she almost fell for this. "I just shouldn't show up then?"

"No, I didn't say that. You should still go, with backup of course. I have an idea of what we could do." At that point, Ed began to list of his admittedly hastily put together plan.

———————◉———————

THE NIGHT WAS CLOAKED in a shroud of darkness as Kaylee cautiously slipped out of her hotel room, her footsteps light and deliberate. She cast a furtive glance around the dimly lit corridor, ensuring that no prying eyes lingered nearby. Satisfied that the coast was clear, she made her way towards the elevator, her heart pounding in her chest.

As she approached the reception desk, Kaylee offered a polite nod to the night clerk, who returned her greeting with a warm smile.

"Do you need anything ma'am?" the clerk asked politely.

"Just taking a night stroll. If anyone ask, I just went out for a drink", Kaylee replied with a deceptive grin. The clerk knew that there was something else in her mind but this matter did not concern her. However, the clerk's hand moved to grab the reception phone.

The security guard stationed near the entrance gave Kaylee a nod of recognition, his presence a reassuring presence in the quiet lobby, one which Kaylee wished she could take around but unfortunately, he didn't work for her. She wondered if she should hire a security person. Would that help though? How would she pay him anyway?

With a sense of urgency gnawing at her insides, Kaylee stepped out into the cool night air and broke into a steady jog. The rhythmic sound of her footsteps echoed against the deserted streets as she made her way through the city, her senses sharp and alert. It was almost midnight, but from far away, she could still see opened restaurants, people driving to parties, a wonderful sound of jazz music coming from a small African antique store that was barely a stone throw away from the hotel and the clacking sounds of bicycle chains as a delivery boy rode down the street to drop of pizza's. Delivery boy? She didn't see the face, why'd she assume that it's a boy. Kaylee shook her head and decided to get back in focus. She had a mission this night.

As she reached the edge of town, Kaylee found herself crossing a long bridge that stretched out over the river below. The sound of her footfalls mingled with the soft rush of water below, creating a soothing symphony that enveloped her in a cocoon of calm.

But her peace was short-lived. A flicker of movement caught her eye, and Kaylee's heart skipped a beat as she realized she was being followed. Adrenaline surged through her veins as she quickened her pace, the rhythmic pounding of her footsteps drowned out by the pounding of her heart.

With each passing moment, the figure behind her drew closer, their footsteps echoing in her ears like the ominous beat of a drum. Panic clawed at her insides as she realized she was being pursued by not one, but two individuals now.

Desperate to escape, Kaylee veered off the main road and ducked into a nearby park, her breath coming in ragged gasps as she sprinted through the empty pathways. But her pursuers were relentless, their shadows looming ever closer with each passing second.

Suddenly, Kaylee stumbled over a protruding tree root and went sprawling onto the ground, her heart pounding in her chest as she scrambled to her feet. But before she could regain her bearings, the two figures closed in on her, their faces twisted into cruel sneers as they advanced.

Fear coursed through her veins as Kaylee lashed out, her fists connecting with flesh as she fought tooth and nail to defend herself. But her assailants were strong, now matter how hard she tried, there was just no escaping them. Kaylee swung a fist as hard as she could to the man standing right in front of her, it connected with his face, smashing right between his eyes and sending him to the ground. He couldn't even yell, he was passed out. The other man saw this and took correction, he stationed himself properly and held down both her hands. Using his head, he gave her such a powerful smash that she fell on the ground.

Just when it seemed as though all hope was lost, a sudden flurry of movement caught her eye. A figure emerged from the darkness, wielding a bat with lethal precision as he launched himself at her attackers.

With a fierce battle cry, the newcomer swung the bat with all his might, striking one of the assailants squarely in the head. The man crumpled to the ground with a groan, his body limp and lifeless as he lay sprawled on the pavement.

Breathing heavily, Kaylee looked to see Ed standing over her, his eyes blazing with fury as he surveyed the scene before him. Without a word, he scooped her up in his arms and carried her to safety, his presence a comforting anchor in the midst of chaos.

"Are you okay?" Ed cried out?

"I don't think so", Kaylee replied as blood dripped down her face from her hair.

"What are you doing here?"

"I wanted to meet Caroline, I was gonna get one of those hidden cameras for tomorrow's meeting with Elton Mock. Do you think he did this?"

"I don't know. But right now, we need to get you to a hospital."

Together, they stumbled through the deserted streets, their footsteps echoing in the stillness of the night as they made their way towards the nearest chemist. As they disappeared into the darkness, Kaylee couldn't help but feel a surge of gratitude for the man who had come to her rescue.

THE HOSPITAL CORRIDORS buzzed with activity as Kaylee was wheeled into the emergency room, her face pale and drawn with pain. Ed hovered anxiously by her side, his brow furrowed with worry as he watched the medical staff bustle around her.

As the nurse began to clean and dress Kaylee's wounds, Ed took a seat beside her bed, his eyes never leaving her.

"Are you Okay?" he asked softly, his voice laced with concern.

Kaylee nodded weakly, her gaze drifting to the ceiling as she tried to push aside the memories of the harrowing ordeal she had just endured. "I'll be fine, glad they didn't ruin my face," she murmured, her voice barely above a whisper.

Ed reached out to squeeze her hand gently, offering her a small but reassuring smile.

"You were lucky," he said quietly, his tone tinged with relief. "If I hadn't shown up when I did..."

Kaylee's eyes flickered with gratitude as she turned to look at him. "Thank you," she whispered, her voice trembling with emotion. "I don't know what I would have done without you."

Ed's expression softened, his gaze filled with warmth as he returned her gaze. "You don't have to thank me," he said softly. "I'll always be here for you, Kaylee. No matter what."

"Who do you think sent those guys? I didn't even think anyone knew I was outside."

"Really, no one at all knew that you were out of your hotel room at night?"

Kaylee thought for a second. "I mean, non that I know off. I just waved at the clerk and the security but I was careful not to be seen. It couldn't possibly be them right?"

"Well, we can't rule it out. I mean the hotel was paid for by Mr. Mock right? They could be working for him. He is a billionaire after all."

"But why would Elton Mock want to beat me up if he wants to meet me tomorrow?"

"Well, I'm not saying he sent them, but I'm also not ruling that out. Inviting you over could probably just be plan B or he has nothing to do with this and this was just some plot by some Elton Mock fans or some really bad sexist men who don't want to see a woman play for their favorite team."

"Why would anyone do that?"

"Jealousy, thoughtful hate, lots of reasons. But what are you gonna do thought?"

Kaylee reclined back on the hospital chair, recounting her thoughts and wondering what her next step would be. She could use a phone to record and just hope that voice proof could help, assuming that Mr. Mock actually tries to make advances tomorrow. She was just going to clean up, make it seem like nothing happened and go of to meet him. If he did send the thugs, then he'd be in for a surprise.

"I'm going to meet Elton Mock tomorrow."

Ed smiled. "I was hoping you wouldn't give up."

Their conversation was interrupted by the nurse, who had finished tending to Kaylee's wounds and now turned to face them.

"I couldn't help but overhear," she said, her voice quiet but firm. "And I couldn't help but actually wonder... if it was Elton Mock who sent those men after you."

Kaylee and Ed exchanged a startled glance, their minds reeling with the implications of her words.

"Elton Mock?" Kaylee echoed, her voice barely a whisper. "Do you know him?"

"Know him? I used to work for him," she began, her voice tinged with bitterness. "Back in Philadelphia, before he moved here to Boston. I was his personal nurse. He'd always come back with some kind of injury when he went gliding or golfing. He... he tried to take advantage of me once, when I was treating his wounds after an accident on the golf course."

Kaylee's eyes widened in shock as she listened to the nurse's story, her heart pounding in her chest as she tried to process the magnitude of what she was hearing. "But why didn't you say anything?" she asked softly, her voice filled with compassion.

The nurse shook her head sadly, her eyes clouded with regret. "I wanted to," she admitted. "But I was scared... and ashamed. I didn't think anyone would believe me."

Ed reached out to place a comforting hand on her shoulder, his expression filled with sympathy. "You don't have to be afraid anymore," he said gently. "We believe you, and we'll do everything we can to make sure justice is served."

"That's the problem, I'm not sure I want that anymore. Maybe for you but, not for me."

"Come on, your testimony could validate everything we're trying to do. You could save a lot more women if you helped us."

The nurse breathed a deep sigh, she was absolutely unprepared for this.

"I'm sorry but... I really want to leave that part of my life behind. It was a very long time ago and I'm willing to forget it. But thank you, for believing me. I wish you good luck in that which you pursue."

The nurse offered them a grateful smile before turning to leave the room, her footsteps echoing in the empty hallway as she disappeared from view. Kaylee and Ed were now left alone in the quiet confines of the hospital room, many thoughts loomed over them.

THE NEXT DAY, KAYLEE once again found herself at the spring home of Elton Mock. "Ugggg", Kaylee said in disgust. "Why did she agree to this again?"

Before she could think of any more vulgar thoughts to describe Elton Mock, the door opened, revealing the man himself.

"Ahhhh, Kaylee, you made it, please, come in. You are right on time. I am impressed."

"Yeah, thanks, it's no problem," Kaylee said this with an undisguised disgust, though Elton failed to notice it.

"Wonderful, follow me."

Kaylee did as requested and followed Elton down a hall and into a large living room area. The furniture looked expensive, and she wondered what it was all really made of.

"Please, have a seat."

"Ok." Kaylee was not thrilled, and was beginning to regret coming.

Elton took his seat in his armchair. "Tea, coffee, or water?"

"No thanks, I just want to get down to business."

"Ah, expeditious. I like that."

"You said you had an offer", Kaylee said, cutting right to the chase.

"Yes, but how bad do you want it?"

"Excuse me?"

"I have doubts, I feel like you're not ready for this. So how bad do you want it?"

Kaylee remained silent as surveyed the room, she realized how much interest Mr. Mock had for expensive things. The expansive living room exuded opulence and grandeur, with soaring ceilings adorned with intricate crown molding and sparkling chandeliers casting a soft, golden glow across the room. Plush, velvet sofas and over sized armchairs upholstered in rich, jewel-toned fabrics beckoned guests to sink into their luxurious embrace. A grand piano stood elegantly in one corner, its polished ebony surface reflecting the warm light from the fireplace, which crackled merrily against a backdrop of marble columns. Ornate Persian rugs sprawled across the gleaming hardwood floors, adding a touch of old-world charm to the contemporary elegance of the space. Large windows draped in heavy silk curtains framed sweeping views of the manicured gardens outside, completing the picture of refined sophistication.

Kaylee nodded, satisfied with her thoughts. He was a man who like good things and he'd do anything to get them. She recognized some of the materials in the room as furnishings you couldn't easily come across. He was truly a go getter and would stop at nothing to get what he wants. Which would validate her next move.

"This much!"

Kaylee stood to her feet and began to walk out of the room leaving the man in awe, she was completely unbothered about the outcome of her walking out on him.

"Alright wait," Mr. Mock said genuinely. "Please sit down, I'll get straight to it."

Kaylee looked around again with a stern frown on her face. She had applied a little make up to perfectly hide the small injuries on her face. She walked over to the chair and sat down gracefully in a comfortable position.

"You had an offer for me?" Kaylee said with a demanding tone.

"Yes, I would like to offer you a position back on the team, if you would be willing."

"What's the catch?", Kaylee asked flatly.

"Oh no catch, just, I need you to do something for me. Some quid pro quo so to speak."

"I believe that is the exact definition of there being a catch", Kaylee said back, not wanting to put up with Elton's bullshit.

"Hmm, yes, I suppose it is. What I want is for you to discredit Ed Oakley, and your teammates at their little press conference."

"And why would I do that?"

It was at this moment that mock did something truly unexpected. He slammed his fist into a Sid table, breaking it into splinters. "DAMN IT, GIRL", Elton yelled. "ISN'T THIS EXACTLY WHAT YOU WANT! TO BE THE FIRST FEMALE MLB PLAYER? I'M GIVING YOU THAT OPPORTUNITY ONCE AGAIN!"

Kaylee did not flinch at this, and instead sat there calmly. Then without missing a beat, simply said, "I just want to play baseball."

A look of confusion came onto Elton's face. Why would anyone not want to play this sport for fame, glory, or money. That answer made no sense to him.

"Please," Elton said, but immediately regret it. "Just discredit the men, just say that everything they've ever said about me is not true and you're back on the team. It's really not that hard."

"You're asking me to embarrass the people that were there for me when you threw me away and you're sitting here telling me it's not that hard. What is wrong with you? How do you live with yourself?"

"Happily. Without regrets. Because unlike the rest of you I'm willing to fight, and I will not let anyone bring me down."

This did not even make sense to Kaylee. She sat down calmly thinking he had more to say but Elton just laid back on the sofa waiting for his answer.

"All my life, I've always only wanted to play baseball, and for this team. I just wake up one day and I'm in that team and then I wake up the next day to find out I'm not here because of my skill, but because of my looks. I've waited over two decades for this. What makes you think I won't wait another decade to find a team owner that really believes in me, while I watch Oakley and your dear team bring you down to your knees?"

Mr. Mock laid back breathing hard, he was furiously clinching his fist and wishing that he could tear her apart. He hoped for her sake and his that her next words would be favorable to both of them.

"However to answer your question, I'll do it", Kaylee continued.

"Really?" Elton said with a quickly switched expression.

"Yes, but on one condition", Kaylee said coldly.

"This isn't a negotiation," Elton said, his voice filled with venom.

"It is is one if you want to get what you want."

Elton crossed his face and pouted like a three year old. "Fine, what is it?"

"You have to be at the press conference as well."

Elton scoffed. "That's it?"

"That's it", Kaylee confirmed. "I will make an announcement at said conference after everyone else has gone. That way it has its best effect."

"But why do you want me to be there?"

"It will help if you're there. Quit asking me questions, are you gonna be there or not?"

"Deal", Elton said, holding out his hand, which Kaylee shock. "See you tomorrow Ms. Dyer", Elton said cheerfully.

Kaylee stood to her feet again to leave just as the two burly men walked in, but this time, she stopped as she stood over Mr. Mock.

"Did you send some thugs to beat me up?"

"What? Why would I do that?"

"So you didn't send two men to beat me up last night?" she said again as she turned to look at the two men standing by him.

"No, I did not. And in case that is what you're insinuating, these guys were with me at an auction, where I just purchased the painting of the City Outside the Window," Mr. Mock said as he gestured to a large painting by the wall of a little girl locked in a tower and staring at the large and illuminated city outside, which she could not reach.

Kaylee nodded, a deceptive grin written on her face and she smiled satisfyingly.

"Good, cuz if you did, I just want you to know that Ed beat them both a bat."

One of the men shrugged at this.

"Nice painting," Kaylee finalized. With that, she turned and left the mansion. Her and Ed's plan were already unfolding beautifully. She couldn't wait for tomorrow to see Elton's face.

Chapter 9

Execution

The amount of people who showed up for the press conference was staggering, and unnerving at the same time. It made no sense to the players of the Red Hawks, considering they regularly played in loud stadiums with thousands of fans. But this, this was different, and every player present knew why.

The team was even more surprised when Kaylee of all people showed up, and things just got weirder when it turns out Elton Mock himself was in the audience. Most people would say that it would make things more complicated, but for the Red Hawks, it oddly seemed to make things better. It felt like someone was there watching them, encouraging them, but they didn't know who or why. What they did know however was that everything was about to change.

"So?" Little John asked. "Who should deliver the news?"

"I'll go," Mark Wats declared. The others agreed, glad that they didn't have to do it and gave him a nod.

"Thank you," almost everyone else backstage said.

Mark stepped up to the microphone and cleared his throat. "Thank you for coming everyone. As you know, this will be an eventful day, and we felt it was important that you hear directly from us what is happening."

A hush fell over the crowd and reporters began writing furiously on their note pads. "I am sad to announce that after careful thought, that I am leaving the Red Hawks and will not play this season."

There was a great gasp among the audience, and a murmuring could be heard.

"Are you sure this is a good idea?" One teammate asked, suddenly having second thoughts.

"It is the right thing to do", said Little John.

"I am sure you have all by know heard the tale of the first female MLB player, Kaylee Dyer in-promptly quitting her spot on the team. I have since found out however the truth of the situation, and wish to share this with you. It has come to my attention that Ms. Dyer did not quit the team, but was in fact fired after refusing sexual advances from the team owner Elton Mock."

The entire room went silent at this. No one was expecting this at all, and a look of panic crossed the face of Elton Mock. It appears what ever he was expecting, it wasn't this.

Mark continued. "As such, we have all unanimously voted to resign from the team. Suddenly all the other players walked onto the stage, and it soon became evident that the only player who was not there was Daryl Rogers. There were some murmurs, but were quickly shut down when Kaylee herself took the podium.

"I can confirm the allegation against Mr. Mock is indeed true..."

Suddenly and with out warning, Mr, Mock stood up and yelled at Kaylee, "THAT WAS NOT THE DEAL YOU BITCH." There were gasps from the audience, the idea that a well respected business man would do such allegations, and to do more in front of reporters was almost unthinkable. Kaylee for her part remained as composed as a rock.

"If you remember Mr. Mock, I only agreed to speak today, I never agreed to say what you tried to bribe me to say."

"Bribe you? I never tried to bribe you," Mr. Mock yelled back.

"You offered me back a position on the team if I discredit the words of Ed Oakley and the baseball players. But you did try to get me to sleep with you after only my first week on the team..."

"You can't prove that!"

"You're right, but I can prove this," Kaylee said as she pulled out her phone and played a recording of their last conversation, starting from the moment where he made the offer.

"That could have been anybody," Mr. Mock spat out. "You're trying to frame me. Do you know who I am?"

"A misogynistic asshole that's for sure. It's over for you Mr. Mock, neither I, nor any woman will ever be a victim of your unlawful cravings anymore."

Elton looked nervous as this dawned at him, before this turned into pure fury. Against all logic, the man charged the stage. It was not until the billionaire was tackled by 24 professional baseball players that he realized his mistake. Several journalists had jumped up as well, and were either frantically taking notes, or takings and video, some with their cell phones.

"This isn't over, you here me. This isn't over!" Mr. Mock kept yelling out as the players held him down. His face was burning with fury and his fist clenched hard to tear her apart.

She had gotten him, he knew this, but they weren't done just yet.

A couple of minutes later, police arrived along with paramedics, who took him both into custody for assault, and to the hospital for treatment.

It would not take long before the rest of the media outside the sports world would pick up the story, and it was everywhere.

Kaylee had finally done it, Elton Mock was out of her life for good, though that still left quite a few other issues out and unanswered.

———⟐———

KAYLEE WAS IN THE MIDDLE of packing her stuff in the hotel room when suddenly she got a phone call, it was Ed.

"Turn on the TV to ESPN", he said hurriedly before hanging up again.

Kaylee shrugged, did as instructed and was shocked at what she saw.

The screen showed a man in a suit standing in front of a wall made up of MLB logos.

"— as a result of our internal investigation, the team owners across the league have voted to force Mr. Mock to sell the Boston Red Hawks. This decision does not come lightly, but in the light of recent events, we decided it was necessary. In 30 days time, the new owner of the team will be determined through auction, and a press conference will be held to announce the winner and the details of the sale.

"Again, that was MLB commissioner Ed Oakley senior making the determination of misconduct in the Elton Mock scandal. This comes upon earlier news this week that Mr. Mock was facing additional scrutiny by the SEC—", Kaylee turned the TV off.

"Ed Oakley sr. Huh?" She should have known by their shared looks. She shook her head then she returned to packing.

Kaylee was nearly done packing when her phone rang, this time the call was from Mel.

"Hello?" Kaylee answered the phone, wondering why he was calling.

"Hello, it's Mel, and the team is holding a meeting today."

"O.K, I'm still not part of the team?" Kaylee stated bluntly.

"It's about that actually. We would like you back on the team."

Kaylee's eyes bulged. "Is that even your decision to make?"

"We don't care if it is or isn't. It's either that or they hire an entire new team."

Kaylee's eyes swelled up at the thoughts of her teammates doing this for her.

"Thank you", she croaked out.

"No problem, now get yourself down here. We have much to talk about." With that, Mel hung up. A wide smile was on Kaylee's face as she got ready and headed out the door.

AS KAYLEE STEEPED INTO the locker room, her heart pounded with nervous anticipation. She was greeted by the sight of her teammates including, Mel, Little John, and Mark, all seated together, chatting animatedly. The atmosphere was warm and welcoming, except for the absence of Daryl, who had always and still harbored resentment towards her.

Taking a deep breath, Kaylee approached the group, her apprehension palpable. However, any fears she had quickly dissipated as her teammates greeted her with open arms. They exchanged smiles and fist bumps, making her feel instantly at ease.

As they waited together for the coach to arrive, Kaylee felt a sense of camaraderie amongst them. Despite their differences, they were all united by their love for the game and their shared goal of winning.

Finally, the coach walked in, a smile playing on his lips as he held a writing pad in his hand. His presence filled the room with a sense of excitement and anticipation. Kaylee's heart skipped a beat as she awaited his words. She hoped that this was as good as what Mel had told her on the phone.

"Good morning everyone, Kaylee," The coach started, nodding his head at Kaylee. "It has been a crazy week, yeah? That's okay, we're strong, we can make that up. First of all, I'd like to say thank you for agreeing to sign back with the team, the team is nothing without you. Secondly, I'd like to apologize to all of you and most especially to the female amongst us. As a good team manager, it is my duty to tend to the needs of my players as it pertains to this team. And for not paying attention to that, I am sorry, I truly am."

Kaylee nodded, a gesture showing that she accepted his apology. Just then, Daryl walks in and obnoxiously walks past the team manager to sit with the others. The team manager refuses to pay attention to this in the hope of keeping the moment as a good one.

"I hope that we can continue to work together, I hope that we will forget all of this drama, now that it's all over and focus on what's important. We're a family guys, we are. We must accept each other, we must support each other. Your burdens are my burdens, as mine are yours. We must be there when the other one needs us. As we head back to Boston, keep it in my mind, the season has just started, we're not only going to need each other, but we're gonna need the best in each other. So have some rest, get some muscles on, it's gonna be a tough season boys."

The room remained silent for a while until Little John decided to break the silence. "That was a terrible speech but I'm gonna clap anyway since you put in effort." Little John then proceeds to clap out loud, the others join him and laugh at the same time. The team manager chuckles at this, then shakes his head and walks out.

"See you kids in Boston."

<hr>

ELTON MOCK WAS HAVING a terrible week. It had all started out so well, and now he was facing financial fraud charges, was being forced to sell the Red Hawks, and his public reputation was ruined. Even worse, his deal with San Antonio fell through, with them quoting "not wanting to be associated with a possible criminal and toxic individual." Hah, no one would have found out about that stuff if it weren't for Kaylee Dyer. Why had he even hired her in the first place? She wasn't special. He was a genius who would save humanity, only he alone could do this, but eggs needed to be broken along the way,

In Elton's mind, he did no wrong, and was always right. He was unable to comprehend that perhaps what happened to him was indeed his fault.

He was currently confined to his home and was on bail, having been deemed a flight risk. This was something he could agree with the judge about, as he actually agreed with this assessment.

"Mr. Mock, are you listening?", his lawyer asked, who was a balding man sitting across from him in a rather expensive suit.

Elton blinked and was brought back to reality.

"Sorry, I was thinking. You were saying?"

The lawyer looked annoyed. "I was asking, how would you like to proceed. Your options are rather limited."

"How so?" Elton asked, it being obvious to the lawyer the man hadn't been paying attention.

"Well, they got you 100 percent on the assault charges, there's no avoiding them at all."

"You sure about that, I mean media can be manipulated..." the lawyer held up a hand.

"Too many witnesses, the prosecution has plenty to chose from. If you plead guilty, you can probably get away with anger management classes and a fine."

"Ugggg, fine", Elton said, clearly not happy. "What about the forced sale, can we at least fight that?"

"Unfortunately no, they have every right to do what they did. In was in the contract you signed when you originally bought the team as well"

"We should do it anyway", Elton declared.

"Sir. Don't think that the best we...."

"Once I code something, we do it. Do you understand?"

The lawyer sighed. "Of course sir. Please be warned an appointed receiver will have control of the team during this process, and you will have no actual influence over it."

"Oh. But... wouldn't that destroy the value without me in charge."

"Uh, I'm not actually paid to answer that question, though I can tell you that is not a valid legal defense."

Elton moped a little bit more, and sat back on his couch. This was just getting worse and worse. "What about the SEC?"

"No charges have been formally filed, so I can only recommend cooperation with their investigation. If you plan to do anything else, I wasn't here. They don't have any proof for now, but it may not take them long to get one."

"Of course," Elton said. He really wished he had a distraction right now, Like a fire, or aurora borealis. He took a deep breath, well, might as well continue.

THE AIR IN THE AIRPORT terminal hummed with the bustling energy of travelers as the Red Hawks team gathered near the departure gate, their bags packed and their minds focused on the upcoming season. Excitement buzzed through the air as they chatted animatedly amongst themselves, their anticipation palpable as they prepared to board the plane back to Boston. They had an upcoming game at their home stadium and since everyone was back on board and the whole drama had died down, they had to be ready and put in their best. Winning the first game of the season at the home stadium was almost a rule for every major league baseball team, and even every other team in the sport industry.

But amidst the flurry of activity, a sense of urgency crackled in the air as Ed suddenly burst through the crowd, his face pale and stricken with worry. Without a moment's hesitation, he made a beeline for Kaylee, his voice urgent as he delivered the shocking news.

"Kaylee," he gasped, his breath coming in short, ragged bursts. "It's your friend, Caroline... she's been in an accident."

Kaylee's heart plummeted as she processed the words, her mind reeling with disbelief and fear.

"What happened?" Kaylee yelled out inquisitively.

"She thought she could find you at the hotel, she said she had something very important to tell you. When she didn't find you, she thought she could catch up with you at the airport but a truck smashed into the taxi, it flipped over and now she's in the emergency unit."

Her heart skipped a beat. Caroline, her dear friend and confidante, was in danger, and there was no time to waste.

Without a second thought, Kaylee abandoned her bags and began to push her way through the throngs of people, her heart pounding in her chest as she fought against the tide of bodies. Her teammates, Mel, Mark, and Little John, followed close behind, their expressions grim with concern as they hurried to keep pace with her.

As they reached the exit, Kaylee's frustration boiled over, her thoughts consumed by the need to reach Caroline's side as quickly as possible.

"We have to go to the hospital," she declared, her voice trembling with urgency. "Caroline needs us."

Mel nodded solemnly, his brow furrowed with worry as he surveyed the scene before them. "We'll catch the next flight to

Boston," he said firmly, his tone leaving no room for argument. "But right now, your friend needs us more than ever."

With a sense of purpose driving them forward, the group dashed out into the cool night air, their footsteps echoing against the pavement as they raced towards the waiting taxi cabs. The city lights blurred into a kaleidoscope of color as they sped through the streets, the urgency of their mission propelling them ever forward.

As they arrived at the hospital, Kaylee's heart clenched with fear at the sight of the bustling emergency room, its corridors filled with doctors and nurses rushing to and fro. With a sense of determination burning within her, she pushed her way through the crowded waiting area, her eyes scanning the faces of the medical staff until she spotted Ed spotted Caroline's doctor.

"Doctor! Sir! Is she going to be okay?" Ed demanded, his voice trembling with emotion as he clung to the hope that Caroline would pull through.

The doctor hesitated for a moment before speaking, his expression grave. "It's touch and go," he admitted, his voice laced with concern. "But we're doing everything we can to stabilize her."

With a heavy heart, Kaylee sank into a nearby chair, her mind swirling with a whirlwind of emotions as she waited for news of Caroline's condition. Beside her, Mel, Mark, and Little John stood vigil, their silent support a comforting presence in the midst of uncertainty.

As the hours dragged on, the tension in the air grew thick with anticipation, each passing moment stretching into an eternity of waiting. And as the darkness began to filter through the hospital windows, a sense of hope blossomed within Kaylee's heart, her prayers for Caroline's recovery echoing in the quiet of the dark night hours. They all stood still, no one said a word for a long time until Kaylee eventually slept off.

———◆———

THE MORNING SUN PAINTED streaks of gold across the sky as the city slowly stirred to life outside the hospital walls. Inside the room where Caroline lay, Kaylee and Ed sat vigil by er bedside, their faces etched with worry as they waited for her to awaken.

Time seemed to stretch on endlessly, each minute feeling like an eternity as they watched over their friend, willing her to open her eyes and return to them. The soft beeping of the heart monitor provided a steady rhythm in the background, a reminder of Caroline's fragile state.

And then, finally, Caroline's eyelids fluttered open, her gaze unfocused as she blinked against the harsh light of the room. Kaylee's heart skipped a beat as she reached out to gently grasp Caroline's hand, relief flooding through her at the sight of her friend stirring.

"Caroline," Kaylee breathed, her voice thick with emotion. "You're awake."

Caroline managed a weak smile, her voice barely above a whisper as she spoke. "Kaylee... Ed," she murmured, her words tinged with exhaustion. "Thank you for being here."

"I've got you, Caroline," Kaylee said softly. "I'm so sorry about what happened. Who would try to this to you?"

"Who else. If not Elton Mock?" Ed replied, with an angry stare.

"It was an accident really," Caroline replied.

"No way, this was his doing. I know it. He's angry because we finally got him and brought him down. You know this man did this. What I just don't understand is how he always knows where to find us. It's like he has people watching us."

"What was it you were going to tell me?" Kaylee asked in a gentle tone.

Caroline took a deep sigh, not sure she should be saying what she wanted to say. She had been through a lot already and didn't really want anything to come at her again. But it had already happened, what more could possibly happen? Mr. Mock, if it was indeed him, had already tried to hurt her, she would not miss the opportunity to hurt him too.

"I spoke with Mr. Mock's lawyer..."

Kaylee's heart clenched at the mention of Mock, her mind racing with the implication of his potential threats. If he was willing to harm Caroline, whom Kaylee thought he had no idea, what lengths would he go to in order to protect his own interests?

"We need to stop him," Caroline continued, her voice growing stronger with determination. "He wants to harm you, and Ed and the team. He's gonna come for everybody. It's not over. The only way... is to find proof... of his crimes... money laundering... tax fraud. This way, he'll be behind bars... all his wealth and properties will be seized... he won't have access to anything or anyone he can use to cause problems. I have a..."

Before Caroline could elaborate further, the door swung open, and a black nurse named Bianca entered the room, her expression stern as she instructed Kaylee and Ed to step outside. With a heavy sigh, they reluctantly complied, their hearts heavy with worry for Caroline's well-being.

As they waited anxiously in the hallway, a sense of unease settled over them, the minutes stretching into an agonizing eternity as they strained to hear any sign of Caroline's condition. And then, suddenly, the silence was shattered by the sound of frantic voices, followed by the urgent summons of a doctor. The black nurse rushed out of the room and began yelling out for other nurses and doctors.

Kaylee's heart plummeted as she exchanged a panicked glance with Ed, her thoughts consumed by hear for Caroline's safety. Without a second thought, they rushed back into the room, only to be stopped in their tracks by the grim faces of the medical staff.

"She's convulsing," a nurse answered. "Just let us do our jobs." The nurse closed the curtains and went back into the room just as the black nurse stepped out with a syringe and walked past them towards the end of the hallway. Kaylee stared at her, wondering why she was acting so suspicious but was too teary and frustrated to ask questions.

Time passed, seconds into minutes and the medical staff where still not done. Kaylee had her fingers crossed together and praying out loud. Suddenly, the room became silent as midnight, all they could hear were quiet footsteps of the medical staff in the room, backed by suspicious whispers between themselves. Then, the doctor stepped out first.

"What's happening?" Kaylee demanded, her voice trembling with fear as she she searched the doctor's eyes for answers.

The doctor hesitated for a moment, his expression somber as he delivered the devastating news. "I'm sorry," he said softly, his words heavy with sorrow. "Caroline... she's gone."

A wave of shock and disbelief washed over Kaylee as she struggled to comprehend the enormity of the loss, her mind reeling with grief and shock. Tears welled in her eyes as she thought of a world without her dear friend by her side.

Beside her, Ed's hand found hers, his touch a silent comfort in the face of overwhelming sorrow. Together, they clung to each other, their grief intertwining as they mourned the loss of a beloved friend.

Outside the hospital room, the world continued to spin on, oblivious to the pain and sorrow within its walls. Nurses bustled about their duties, patients shuffled through the corridors, and life carried on as it always did.

"She wasn't even a nurse," Kaylee said amidst tears.

"Who wasn't a nurse?" Ed asked, his voice trailing with sorrow.

"The woman that came in. Didn't you see. She left immediately they came in."

"Maybe resuscitation isn't her job."

"No, I saw it in her eyes. She was scarred, and nervous. They didn't even recognize her. I think she killed Caroline. I think Mr. Mock sent her here to kill Caroline."

"Come on Kaylee, that is quite an accusation."

"I don't care! You know it's the truth!" Kaylee yelled out. "And speaking of truth, when were you gonna tell me that your father is the head of the MLB?

Is there anything else you're not telling me? Is your name even Ed Oakley?"

"No!" Ed replied quietly, his resolve still maintained calmly.

"What?"

"Mr. Oakley is my step day. My real dad is late Mr. Berneth. I am Ed Benet but since I was adopted by Mr. Oakley, I decided to take on his name so I wouldn't be reminded everyday of how my father died."

"I'm so sorry. I got angry."

"It's okay. We'll get through this you know, together. Mr. Mock hurt badly, a long time ago. I haven't been able to forgive him since then. I just want to see him go down, for everything he's done, not just to me but to everyone else he's ever tried to hurt. If what it will take is us finding proof of his illegal dealings, then I'll do it, no matter what it takes."

Kaylee turned to look at him, she felt a revitalization flow through her blood. She swung her arm around Ed and dragged him closer. Feeling his body over hers somehow made her feel better.

"Thank you."

<hr />

AS KAYLEE FINISHED her meal, she couldn't shake the memories of Caroline, Ed Oakley, and the terrifying events in Florida. Despite being back in Boston and the warm embrace of her simple Boston apartment, the events of recent days weighed heavily on her mind as she settled down to watch some television before bed.

The television flickered with the news, but Kaylee's attention wandered. She kept replaying the vents of the past few days in her mind, unable to escape the feeling of impending danger that seemed to linger around every corner. She knew she had to stay vigilant, but exhaustion gnawed at her bones, pulling her closer to sleep with each passing moment.

As the night deepened, a figure clad in a dark outfit moved silently through the suburban streets towards Kaylee's apartment. Their footsteps echoed softly against the pavement, barely audible in the stillness of the night.

Meanwhile, Kaylee drifted off into a fitful sleep, her dreams haunted by shadows and flickers of flame. She tossed and turned, unaware of the danger creeping ever closer to her doorstep.

Suddenly, Kaylee was jolted awake by the acrid smell of smoke. Panic surged through her veins as she leaped out of bed, her heart pounding in her chest. Smoke billowed through the crack beneath her door, thick and suffocating.

With trembling hands, Kaylee fumbled for her phone, dialing 911 as she coughed and choked on the smoke filling her apartment.

"911 what's your emergency?"

"My house is on fire!" Kaylee yelled out at the dispatcher, who seemed not the least concerned.

"Ma'am are you inside the house?" the dispatcher screamed out, finally realizing the desperateness of the situation.

"Yes, I'm trapped inside. Please help me out, I don't wanna die, please, please!," Kaylee cried out, she was already beginning to get sweaty and teared up.

"Alright ma'am, I'll have the fire service on their way to you immediately. Can you please, state your address?" the dispatcher said.

The dispatcher's voice sounded distant and distorted as Kaylee gasped out her address, her words barely coherent over the roar of the flames. "Alright ma'am, please stay calm and find a safe place to hide. I have the police and fire service on their way to you right now."

Outside, neighbors emerged from their homes, drawn by the wall of sirens and the acrid stench of smoke. They watched in horror as flames licked hungrily at Kaylee's apartment, devouring everything in their path.

The local press arrived soon after, their cameras flashing as they captured the chaos unfolding before them. Reporters shouted questions, clamoring for answers amidst the chaos of the scene.

Inside the apartment, Kaylee fought to stay calm as the fire raged around her. Smoke stung her eyes and seared her lungs with each labored breath. Desperate to escape the inferno, she stumbled towards the nearest exit, her vision blurred with tears.

As she reached the basement door, a blast of heat washed over her, driving her to her knees. The roared behind her, a relentless force of destruction that threatened to consume everything in its path. She watched at her living room went up in flames, including her favorite girl stuff and her favorite baseball bat which had been a gift from her late grand dad. She really cherished that bat. But right now, her life was in danger, she was almost seeing death taking over her. She didn't even have the time or energy to think of how all this started.

With trembling hands, Kaylee pushed open the door and stumbled down into the darkness below. The air was thick with smoke, making it difficult to see more than a few feet in front of her.

Suddenly, the floor above her groaned and creaked, sending shards of debris raining down around her. Kaylee's heart pounded in her chest as she realized the building was collapsing around her. She was beginning to loose it, her lungs were almost completely filled with smoke. She was falling slowly as she gradually passed out, all reasoning had left her. She could see and hear patterns right now.

But just as all hope seemed lost, a figure emerged from the smoke, clad in heavy firefighting gear. It was a firefighter, his face obscured by a mask as he rushed towards her through the flames.

With a strength born of desperation, the firefighter hoisted Kaylee into his arms and carried her towards safety. Each step was a struggle against the raging inferno, but he pressed on, determined to get her out alive.

But before he could get to the front door, the roof of the front porch had given up and fallen down the front porch with a loud bang, giving the firemen outside such a scare that they ran back. The whole front was now on fire. The firemen tried hard to spray water over it but it was just too much.

Inside the apartment, it was getting too hot and the firefighter could feel his body giving up. He ran up to the stairs to the top floor, hoping to throw her down to the other fire men but immediately he got to the room upstairs, he had to stop in his steps, realizing that a deep suspicion may just have become real. The firefighter immediately engulfs himself around Kaylee as the floor gave way and crashed down. The firefighter fell below and landed on the glass table, however, he made sure Kaylee wasn't hurt.

He decides to be smart, he grabbed a side of the wall that had fallen and now looked like a stretched out plank, poured a gallon of water from the kitchen over it and then laid it out at the door way. He grabbed her and stood ready, hoping that this idea was a good one and the building wouldn't come crashing down on them once they applied pressure to the doorway. With a surge of adrenaline and determination running in his veins, he dashed out through the front door, Kaylee held strongly in his arms.

Finally, they emerged from the burning building, the cool night air washing over them like a balm. Kaylee gasped for breath, her lungs burning from smoke inhalation as paramedics rushed to her side.

As she was loaded into the waiting ambulance, Kaylee caught a glimpse of the firefighter who had saved her life. His eyes met hers for a brief moment, and in that instant, she saw the silent strength and unwavering determination that had carried them both through the darkest of nights.

But even as she lay in the ambulance, battered and bruised, Kaylee couldn't shake the feeling that this was only the beginning. The events of the past few days had shaken her to her core, and she knew that the danger was far from over. What she didn't know however was what to do next and how she would do it alone.

KAYLEE'S GRAND-SLAM

As the ambulance raced through the streets towards the hospital, Kaylee's thoughts turned to the mysterious figure who had started the fire. Who were they, and what did they want with her? And more importantly, how could she stop them before it was too late? Or did someone send them to her?

But for now, Kaylee pushed those thoughts aside, focusing instead on the gratitude she felt towards the firefighter who had saved her life. She closed her eyes, allowing herself to drift into a fitful sleep as the ambulance sped towards the safety of the hospital. Hopefully this place couldn't go up in flames.

Meanwhile, back at the scene of the fire, firefighters battled tirelessly to extinguish the flames and prevent further damage to the surrounding buildings. The night was long and arduous, but their efforts paid off as the fire was finally brought under control.

As dawn broke over the city, Kaylee's apartment laid in ruins, a charred shell of its former self. But amidst the destruction, there was hope- hope for a new beginning, and hope for a brighter future. And as she drifted into a restless sleep, Kaylee couldn't help but feel a glimmer of despair, but at the same time of hope – hope for a future where she could finally leave the darkness of the past behind and embrace the light of a new day. She was going to find how this was all happening, who was watching her and why they always wanted to hurt her. She had assumed that this was all over and she could return to her normal life, but it seemed to road ahead was still far stretched. She hoped even more at this moment that her team members and Ed were with her.

THE SOFT MORNING LIGHT filtered through the curtains, casting a gentle glow across the hospital room. Kaylee stirred, her head throbbing with pain as she slowly opened her eyes. Beside her, Mel and Little John sat quietly, their faces etched with concern.

"Hey, she's awake," Mel said softly to Little John.

"How are you feeling?" Little John asked softly, his voice filled with genuine worry.

Kaylee managed a weak smile, her head still spinning from the events of the previous night. "I've definitely been better. Feels like there's a drum line rehearsing in my head."

Little John nodded sympathetically. "Yeah, that was quite the hit you took back there. But don't worry, you'll bounce back in no time."

"Mark sent his well wishes, he couldn't be here. He's married," Mel said slowly.

Kaylee chuckled at this. She was grateful for their presence, it felt good to wake up to genuine company from friends who wished her well. As they chatted about her health and the upcoming game against the Philadelphia Bulls, one of the most formidable teams in the baseball league, the team manager entered the room, his expression grave.

"Morning, everyone," he greeted, his tone serious. "I've got some news."

Kaylee's heart sank as she braced herself for what was to come.

"I just had a chat with the doctor, you burns aren't bad, luckily nothing vital was hurt. But there were reports about a fall, she also says that we'll need to put you on certain drugs and make sure to keep you stress free for about a month."

Kaylee was taken back, this couldn't possibly be happening. "A month. It's just a few burns. I feel completely fine."

"Let's not argue with the health people. This is best for you and the team."

"But if I'm off for a month, that means..."

"I've decided to drop you from playing in the next game against the Philadelphia Bulls," he announced, his words hanging heavily in the air.

The news hit her like a ton of bricks. She felt a surge of disappointment and frustration coursing through her veins. This was supposed to be her chance to prove herself, to show the world what she was made of. And now it was being taken away from her.

"What? Why?" Kaylee demanded, her voice tinged with disbelief.

The manager sighed, his expression sympathetic. "Look, I know you're itching to get back out there, but you're not fully recovered yet. We can't risk your health, especially against a tough team like the Bulls."

Kaylee clenched her fists, fighting back the wave of frustration threatening to overwhelm her. She knew he was right, but that didn't make it any easier to accept.

Just then, Ed burst into the room, his eyes wild with concern.

"Kaylee are you okay?" he asked, rushing to her side.

Kaylee's countenance suddenly changed, even though she was shaken about missing the game, she was extremely happy to see Ed. Mel and Little John exchanged a knowing glance before quietly excusing themselves, leaving Kaylee and Ed alone.

"I'm fine," Kaylee replied, forcing a smile despite the disappointment gnawing at her. "Just a little banged up, that's all."

Ed reached out and gently squeezed her hand, his eyes filled with concern. "I heard what happened. I'm so sorry I wasn't there to help."

Kaylee shook her head, her heart swelling with gratitude. "You don't need to apologize. You're here now, and that's all that matters."

They sat in silence for a moment, the weight of the situation hanging heavy in the air.

Chapter 10
Survival

As they stepped into the apartment, Kaylee couldn't help but feel a sense of curiosity mixed with anticipation. They had spent three days in the hospital and through it all, Ed had only left on few occasions to handle business but he made sure he was with her through all of her recovery. She had tired limbs and felt very weak. The doctor had recommend a parade of drugs to sustain her and she had to do physical therapy. She was finally happy to be out of the hospital space and seeing the outside world again, although she wasn't sure where she was. The space was tastefully decorated, with modern furnishings and a warm, inviting ambiance. Soft ambient lighting cast a gentle glow over the room, creating a cozy atmosphere.

"Where are you?" Kaylee asked inquisitively. She couldn't help but feel submerged in the beauty and aura of the room.

"I friend of mine stays here. He's out of town so he's letting us use it for now," Ed responded.

The living room was spacious, with a plush sofa and a pair of comfortable armchairs arranged around a sleek coffee table. A large flat-screen TV adorned one wall, while a collection or art work added a touch of personality to the space. The walls were painted in a soothing neutral tone, accented by pops of color in the form of throw pillows and decorative accents.

Ed led Kaylee further into the apartment, gesturing towards the adjoining bedroom with a smile. "This is the living room," he said, his voice warm and welcoming. "And over there is the bedroom. You can take a shower, there are some lady clothes in the closet. I'll get dinner ready."

Kaylee's eyes widened in surprise as she took in the sight of the bedroom. It was spacious and elegantly furnished, with a king-sized bed dressed in luxurious linens and a cozy throw blanket. A sleek dresser stood against one wall, its surface adorned with a few carefully curated decorative items.

A large window flooded the room with natural light, offering a stunning view of the city skyline. She could see the twinkling lights of the city below, a sight that never failed to take her breath away.

"This apartment is amazing," Kaylee exclaimed, turning to him with a smile. "Thank you so much, for everything."

Ed grinned, his eyes sparkling with warmth. "It's my pleasure, Kaylee," he said. "I'm glad you like it. Make yourself at home."

"How long do we have it?"

"Quite long actually. He's a government contractor, they're building a bridge over some large body of water in Oklahoma. He'll be out for a while."

"I like that," Kaylee said with a tiny chuckle. "What are you gonna cook?"

"Well I'll have to see what's available first."

"Right. I'll just go shower now. Sure you don't wanna join me?" Kaylee said sheepishly as she walked into the room.

"You don't mean that," Ed responded with a grin.

"Nope, but you would if I did, wouldn't you?" Kaylee said a wide smile and seductive eyes as she closed the bedroom door.

After a long and invigorating shower, Kaylee emerged from the bathroom, her skin aglow and her spirits lifted by the refreshing cascade of water. She wrapped herself in a plush towel, relishing the warmth and softness against her skin as she made her way into the living room.

The living room exuded an air of understated elegance, with tastefully arranged furniture and artfully placed decor creating a cozy and inviting atmosphere. Sunlight streamed in through the windows, casting warm golden hues across the room and infusing it with a sense of serenity.

Kaylee's eyes swept over the space, taking in the sleek lines of the furniture, the plush area rug beneath her feet, and the carefully curated artwork adorning the walls. She couldn't but marvel at the room's design again. With a contented sigh, Kaylee made her way into the bedroom, the soft carpeting muffling the sound of her footsteps as she moved. The bedroom was equally inviting, with a sumptuously appointed bed taking center stage and inviting her to sink into its embrace. She wanted to lay on this bed, but not alone. Alone is lonely. She realized that she had not been with a man or dated anyone in almost a decade. She had dedicated her whole life to baseball and didn't even give room for anything else.

She paused for a moment, taking in the sight of the bed with its crisp while linens and plump pillows, a promise of comfort and relaxation after a long day. A sense of anticipation fluttered in her chest as she imagined curling up beneath the covers and drifting off into a peaceful slumber. She deserved it.

But first, Kaylee needed to tend to her post-shower routine. With practiced efficiency, she moved to the dresser and selected a bottle of fragrant lotion, the subtle scent of lavender filling the air as she smoothed it over her skin. The lotion left her skin feeling soft and supple, a welcome indulgence after the rigors of the day.

Next, Kaylee reached for a bottle of perfume, the delicate fragrance wafting around her as she spritzed it lightly over her pulse points. The scene was subtle yet alluring, a lingering reminder of her presence long after she had left the room.

With her skincare routine complete, Kaylee turned her attention to her hair, running a comb through the damp strands and smoothing out any tangles. The mirror reflected her image back at her, the soft glow of the overhead lights illuminating her features and casting a flattering light on her appearance. Satisfied with her appearance, Kaylee wrapped the towel securely around her body and made her way to the closet. But as she opened the door, she was met with a surprising sight- the closet contained only male clothing, a stark reminder of the fact that she was guest in the apartment.

Undeterred, Kaylee reached for the only item of female clothing she could find – a silky night robe- and slipped it on, the luxurious fabric draping elegantly over her curves. Despite the slight discomfort of wearing unfamiliar attire, she couldn't help but feel a sense of feminine allure as she admired her reflection in the mirror.

With her attire sorted, Kaylee padded barefoot into the kitchen, the cool tiles soothing against her skin as she moved. She called out to Ed, but there was no response, prompting her to explore the contents of the kitchen cabinets while she waited for his return.

As she rummaged through the drawers, Kaylee couldn't help but marvel at the array of utensils and gadgets that filled them. Each item seemed to have its place, a testament to the owners meticulous organization and attention to detail.

Suddenly, the sound of the door opening caught her attention and Kaylee turned to see Ed entering the apartment, a bag of groceries in hand. Her heart skipped a beat at the sight of him, his rugged charm and easy smile sending a jolt of warmth through her.

"Hey, Kaylee," Ed greeted, his voice warm and inviting. "I picked up some groceries on the way home. Thought we could whip up something delicious for dinner."

Ed stared down at her, the silky fabric making her skin look brighter as it exposed almost every part of her body. The lights sneaked glances at her finely toned skin as the outfit revealed her curves. Her almost wet her flowed gracefully behind her and presented her, an angel in human skin. It was no wonder a billionaire wanted her.

Kaylee's cheeks flushed at the sight of him, her pulse quickening at the sound of his voice. Despite the initial awkwardness of her attire, she found herself drawn to him, her eyes lingering on his rugged features and broad shoulders.

"Uh, hi, Ed," she replied, her voice slightly breathless. "That sounds great. Let me help you with those."

As Ed set the groceries down on the kitchen counter, Kaylee moved to assist him, her heart fluttering with anticipation at the prospect of spending more time with him. Despite the unfamiliar surroundings and the unexpected turn of events, she couldn't shake the feeling of being exactly where she was meant to be.

As they worked together to organize the groceries, Kaylee and Ed found themselves stealing glances at each other, the air between them crackling with tension. Their hands brushed occasionally as they reached for items, sending sparks of electricity shooting through their bodies.

When Kaylee struggled to reach a box of cereal on the top shelf, Ed stepped in to help without hesitation. Standing behind her, he reached over her shoulder, his tall frame towering over her as he stretched to place the box in its rightful place. But as leaned in close, his body pressed against hers, a wave of heat washed over them both.

Their eyes met, locking in a silent exchange of longing and desire. Kaylee's breath caught in her throat as she felt the warmth of Ed's body against her own, his proximity sending shivers down her spine. For a moment, they lingered in the embrace, the world falling away as they lost themselves in each other's gaze.

Breaking the spell, Kaylee turned and perched herself on the kitchen counter, her eyes smoldering with desire as she traced her fingers teasingly along Ed's chest. Her touch sent a jolt of electricity through him, igniting a firestorm of passion that threatened to consume them both.

"You know," she purred seductively, her voice husky with desire, "the bed seems really soft."

Ed's heart raced at the suggestive tone of her voice, his pulse quickening with anticipation. He got the hint and immediately moved closer to kiss her, but Kaylee placed a finger on his lips to stop him, "Shirt off first." Without hesitation, he shed his shirt, revealing his toned physique beneath the fabric. Kaylee's eyes drank in the sight of him, a hunger burning in her gaze as she reached out to him, her fingers trailing down his chest and lower, teasing the bulge that strained against his pants.

Their bodies pressed together, the heat between them building with each passing moment. With a gentle touch, Ed raised the hem of Kaylee's robe, his fingers tracing the contours of her body as he explored every inch of her skin. She trembled beneath his touch, her breath coming in shallow gasps as she surrendered to the intoxicating sensation of his hands on her.

Their lips met in a searing kiss, their mouths moving hungrily against each other as they gave in to the primal urge that pulsed between them. With each kiss, the flames of desire burned hotter, consuming them in a whirlwind of passion and longing.

Ed's hands roamed freely over Kaylee's body, caressing her curves and igniting a firestorm of sensation that threatened to consume them both. With a gentle thrust, he lifted her into his arms, carrying across the kitchen and into the bedroom with a sense of urgency that mirrored their own desires.

In the dim light of the bedroom, they shed their clothes with reckless abandon, their bodies melding together in a frenzy of need and longing. With each touch, each caress, they explored the depths of their desire, losing themselves in the heady intoxication of their shared passion.

As they tumbled onto the soft, inviting bed, Kaylee spread her legs wide open, inviting Ed to join her in a dance of ecstasy and pleasure. With a hungry look in his eyes, he moved closer, his arousal evident as he prepared to take her to heights of pleasure she had never known. With a whispered promise of ecstasy hanging in the air, Ed closed the door behind them, sealing their newfound intimacy in a cocoon of privacy and seclusion. And as they surrendered to the throes of passion, they lost themselves in each other, their bodies entwined in a symphony of desire that echoed through the night.

———◉———

KAYLEE AND ED STOOD side by side in the spacious kitchen, surrounded by an array of colorful ingredients spread out across the counter top. As they prepared to cook dinner together, the warm glow of the overhead lights cast a cozy ambiance over the room. It had been a busy night, for two of them alone and they were tired but hungry. They had just had their shower and had walked into the kitchen to make a delicious meal for the night.

"So, who do you think could be behind all of this?" Ed asked, his voice tinged with concern as he diced onions with precision. He felt that the time had really just come to ask.

Kaylee furrowed her brow, pondering the question as she carefully measured out spices for their meal. "Honestly, I'm not sure. But something tells me Mr. Mock might be involved. He's always had it out for me."

Ed nodded thoughtfully, his knife pausing mid-air. "Yeah, he really hates you. But he's not the type to get his hands dirty. He probably has someone else doing his bidding. Someone who's close to you."

"I can't really tell anyone else who'd want to see me hurt. But I do believe the part where he has people working for him."

"They don't really need to have a motivation for it. He could just be paying them."

They worked in companionable silence for a few moments, the only sounds in the room the rhythmic chopping of vegetables and the occasional sizzle of ingredients in the pan. But the weight of the conversation hung heavy in the air, casting a shadow over their culinary efforts.

"What about Daryl?" Kaylee interjected, breaking the silence. "He's always had it out for me too. Maybe he's working with Mr. Mock."

Ed's expression darkened at the mention of Daryl's name, his jaw clenched with frustration. "It's possible. You said he's never been your biggest fan. But I'm not convinced he's capable of orchestrating something like this."

"The dude is a large, six foot man who can handle a bat like a German bartender, I feel like he'll be perfect for this."

"Didn't you say Mr. Mock once had him beat up after he wasn't nice to you. Why then would he want to work for Mock."

"Same reason why everyone else would like to work for Mr. Mock, the money. He could be doing all of this to get me kicked out so I don't steal his sport light and still get paid. It's a double win for him."

"He already has money, and I don't mean this offensively but, he is still kinda better than you. I mean he's been in the league for what, eight years?"

"Non taken to the man who's supposed to be supporting me right now," Kaylee yelled out then dropped the knife and turned around in a fume.

Ed walked over to her and held her waist from behind then planted a gentle kiss on her shoulder. "I didn't mean it like it. I'm just saying, I don't think he's the kind to do this kind of stuff, you know?"

Kaylee nodded in agreement, her mind racing with possibilities. "And then there's that nurse in Florida. The one who treated Caroline. I know she killed my best friend."

Ed's eyes narrowed, as he released her and tightened his grip on the knife. "I mean, she did seem off. But we can't jump to conclusions. What we need, is concrete evidence if we're going to take down Mr. Mock once and for all. We need to prove that he is in fact involved in money laundering and tax fraud."

Kaylee sighed, feeling the weight of their predicament bearing down on her. "I know, but how do we even begin to find that evidence? Mr. Mock is too careful to leave any traces behind."

Ed reached out, gently squeezing her hand in reassurance. "We'll figure it out, Kaylee. Together. We just have to stay vigilant and trust our instincts."

As they finished preparing dinner, the tantalizing aroma of their culinary creation filled the kitchen, wrapping them in a comforting embrace. Sitting down at the table, they shared a meal filled with laughter and conversation, momentarily forgetting the challenges that lay ahead.

AS KAYLEE AND ED NESTLED together on the couch, the soft glow of the television casting a warm ambiance in the room, they chatted about their day and the latest happenings in their lives. Their conversation flowed effortlessly, filled with laughter and affectionate teasing.

"So tell me," Ed said. "How exactly is it that you get a tiny ball thrown at you and you use a narrow piece of metal to hit it?"

"Well first of all," Kaylee replied. "The ball isn't tiny. And it's really not easy but you just garra focus. From that moment when the pitcher is attempting to throw, you need to study him, see what he's about to do and hope that you've practiced well enough to know what the pitcher is going to do."

"So there's like trick throws in this game?"

"How are you the son to the MLB chairman and don't know these things?"

"I'm a journalist, there's really not enough time to learn this," Ed replied as he laughed.

"I know a lot of billionaires that know the rules of this game inside and out."

Their conversation was interrupted by the urgent tone of the evening news anchor, capturing their attention as the breaking news segment began and a picture of Kaylee Dyer was hanging by the side of the screen.

"...also in today's news, an allegation has been received from an anonymous source regarding current major league baseball player for the Boston Red Haws, Kaylee Dyer."

Kaylee's heart skipped a beat as she watched the screen, her stomach churning with anxiety. Beside her, Ed tensed, his grip on her hand tightening in concern.

"What's going on?" he asked, his voice laced with worry.

Kaylee shook her head, her mind racing with possibilities. "I don't know, but it can't be good."

The news report unfolded, revealing the allegations of document and academic dishonesty. "An anonymous source has come forward with startling allegations against former college baseball and current major league baseball star, Kaylee Dyer. According to the source, there are claims of document falsification and academic dishonestly during her time in college. These allegations have cast a shadow of doubt over her previous achievements, raising questions about her integrity and eligibility to play professional baseball. Further more, our Channel 9 investigative reporter visited Kaylee Dyer's alma mater, and after thorough inquiries, it's been confirmed that she falsified signatures of her guardians to secure financial aid. This revelation has sent shock waves through the sports community, tarnishing Dyer's reputation and raising serious doubts about her credibility.

Kaylee listened in disbelief, her world spinning as her past achievements were called into question. She turned to see Ed turning to the side with his head buried in his laps.

"It's not true," Kaylee said softly.

"Stop lying to me!" Ed yelled out. "I hoped it wouldn't come out. I even tried to destroy it but my boss wouldn't let me. Why would you lie about this?"

"You knew this whole time?"

"I'm a journalist, Kaylee, it's my job to know these things."

"Did you release it?"

"Oh don't be silly, you know I'd never do that."

"I had no choice. I didn't have a choice," Kaylee said amidst tears in her eyes. She wished he would believe him.

"What do you mean you didn't have a choice. Your parents are not dead Kaylee, neither are they poor."

"You don't understand."

"Of course I don't understand, because you never tell me anything. How many of the things you've told me are even actually true?"

"I have never lied to you and you know it."

"Of course, Kaylee," Ed said and turned to the side, trying to hold down his frustration. He refused to look at her.

"Please talk to your dad, I can't afford to lose this job."

"Seriously, that's your problem right now? Baseball? Does anything else every matter to you? Do you care about anything or anyone else? You left your parents and your best friend for years without one call, not even a text, because of baseball. And now even when it comes down to your dignity, in the presence of the whole world, you're still only concerned about baseball."

"I do care about other things," Kaylee replied, now with tears soiling her face. "I care about other people. I'm just on a very lonely part right now. It's slow and it's dangerous and no matter how much people try to help me, I'm still in it alone, but nobody sees that. It's the one thing I've dreamnt about my whole life, why am I a bad person because I try hard to see that it happens no matter what?"

Ed stayed silent for a while, letting her words sink in, but he wasn't ready to be veered. "Because there are other important things in life, Kaylee. This is why you shut everyone out isn't it? This is why you went to a different college far from home and got a house in the suburbs. You don't care about other people, you think they don't want the best for you. You think everyone is against you following your dreams so you'd just rather stay away from them. That's typical, Kaylee."

Kaylee stared deep into Ed's eyes, surprise written on her face as more tears flowed down. "You're right. I stay away from people because I feel like they're not good for me. I refuse everyone because I feel like they do not support what I want to be. But look at me, look at the past few weeks of my life. Now tell me... Am I wrong?"

With that, Kaylee storms into the corridor and into the bedroom, leaving Ed pondering on many thoughts. She shortly appears again wearing a coat and storms out the room, jamming the door loudly behind her.

Outside the room, Kaylee quickly runs down the stares, wiping her tears with the arms of her jacket. She bumps into a youth carrying groceries and rushes off without apologizing. Kaylee dashes out of the building and immediately hails a taxi, she jumps in and yells at the driver to move. The car screeches in motion and drives out of the scene. Shortly later, Ed runs out of the building and searches around to find her but doesn't see anyone.

As the clock struck midnight, Ed found himself wandering the dimly lit streets of the city, his heart heavy with worry. Desperation drove him forward as he approached strangers, asking if they had seen a woman matching Kaylee's description. Some shook their heads and hurried away, while others simply ignored him, lost in their own worlds.

Ed checked alleys, subways, and bus stations, his footsteps echoing in the empty corridors. Each passing minute felt like an eternity as he searched for any sign of her presence.

His search led him to bars and restaurants, where he scanned the crowds with growing anxiety. But Kaylee was nowhere to be found among the revelers and diners, leaving him feeling more helpless than ever. With every passing moment, Ed's worry grew, gnawing at his insides like a relentless beast. He couldn't bear the thought of Kaylee out there alone, vulnerable to the dangers of the night.

As he turned onto a lonely street, a group of hooded figures emerged from the shadows, their faces obscured by darkness. Ed's pulse quickened as he instinctively tensed, his senses on high alert.

"Hey, what do you want?" Ed demanded, trying to sound confident despite the fear gnawing at his insides.

The figures advanced, their movements predatory and menacing. Ed's heart hammered in his chest as he backed away, searching frantically for an escape route.

"Nah bro, ain't no escaping here," one of the figures called out. "How about you drop your wallet and your phone. And be gone."

"Please, I am trying to find a missing person. I have only thirty dollars in my wallet but if it's soo important to you, you can have it. I just really need the phone to find my girl."

"Did you see any girls on these streets. This is our street bro, ain't no girls around these parts. Now drop the phone and the wallet and get lost," the figure yelled again.

Ed could see that there was clearly no reasoning with them, he turned around to find a route to escape through, but before he could react, the muggers were upon him, their hands grabbing at his pockets with rough, grasping fingers. Panic surged through Ed as he fought back, his adrenaline-fueled instincts kicking into overdrive. Amidst the chaos, a glint of metal caught his eye, and he realized with a sinking feeling that they were truly after his wallet and phone. With a surge of desperation, he lashed out, trying to fend off his attackers as they closed in on him. But it was no use. The muggers were too many, too strong, and Ed found himself overwhelmed by their sheer numbers. In a matter of seconds, they had stripped him of his belongings and left him bruised and battered on the cold pavement.

As he lay there, gasping for breath and nursing his wound, a surge of anger and frustration welled up inside him. How could they do this to him? How could they take everything he had and needed to find Kaylee in an instant? But amidst the pain and confusion, Ed's thoughts turned to Kaylee, and the fear gripped him once again. What if she was out there somewhere, alone and in danger? Probably somewhere, being held down by another group of hood rats. He couldn't even bear the thought of her being hurt because of him. She had already gone through a lot and was still recovering from her wounds.

With a renewed sense of urgency, Ed forced himself to his feet, his limbs aching and his head swimming. He staggered forward, his mind racing with fear and determination, as he searched for any sign of Kaylee in the darkness. But the streets remained empty, the night air eerily silent save for the distant sound of traffic and the occasional shout of a passerby. Ed's heart sank as he realized the futility of his search, the weight of his failure pressing down on him like a physical burden.

And then, just when he thought all hope was lost, he caught sight of a familiar card that had dropped out of his wallet while the boys held him down. He quickly ran over to the end of the alley and picked up, smiling and as glared at the phone number of the card. The owner of that card could most definitely find Kaylee.

Ed ran across the street with renewed energy and at top speed until he found a public phone booth. He quickly got in and looked around, almost scared to not find the hooded boys again. He quickly dialed the numbers on the card, it was a home line. It rang for almost a minute but no one picked up. Ed, refusing to give up, dialed again but no one picked up. He tried again, and again and again but no one picked up until it became excessive and he was ready to give up.

He fell down in the phone booth and just laid there, thinking hard of where to start from. He wished he had not said those words to her. He wished he had just shut up and listened to her. He had forgotten all he had watched her go through. He had also forgotten that all he knew was only what was on record, but never for once had he every bothered to ask her for her side of the story. He was burned with the thought of her wondering the streets of Boston at midnight because she sure wasn't going back to her burnt house. With that, he agreed that he wasn't going to give up until the person picked up. He pushed himself up and dialed the number again and this time, there was a delayed response that came out straight with a yell.

"It's past 1am in the fucking morning, who the fuck is this?"

"Is this the Dyer residence? We have a problem."

———●———

ALONE IN THE DIMLY lit stadium, Kaylee sat curled up in her jacket, the cold night air seeping through the fabric of her jacket. She watched with teary eyes at the whole stadium as if picturing a game in session and she was in the middle of the scene, getting a first glance at everything. She could see players, coaches, managers, an umpire and a large crowd in the small stadium filled with energy as they threw the ball and smashed it into various positions. This was the birth place of her skill, this was the first point of her rejection for baseball. Tears streamed down her cheeks as she stared up at the dark sky, feeling lost and defeated.

"I've tried," she whispered, her voice barely audible over the distant hum of traffic. "I don't understand why nothing seems to go right. What am I doing wrong? Are you even listening, God?"

As if in response, a voice spoke from behind her, sending a shiver down her spine. "No, we did. Everyone else did."

Startled, Kaylee turned to see her father standing there, his presence both comforting and unwelcome at the same time. She hadn't expected to see him here, especially not now, in her moment of vulnerability. But all the same, she wished that someone would be there with her, at least to make her feel safe, and standing right there was there answer to her prayers.

"What are you doing here?" Kaylee asked with a bit of annoyance in her tone.

"I'm your father Kaylee, it's my job to make sure you're not alone," Mr. Dyer replied, a genuine compassion for his daughter evident in his tone.

"How'd you know I'd be here?" she asked, her voice tinged with bitterness.

"Again, I'm your father, Kaylee. I'll always know where you run to," he replied, his tone gentle yet firm. "Although I wish you had come to me instead."

"Definitely not happening, not since I knew I couldn't trust you anymore."

Mr. Dyer sighed, then sat beside her. They both gazed at the stares, wondering whether which would be less awkward, talking to God or to each other.

"What I did..."

"What you and mom did..." Kaylee interrupted.

"No, it was my idea. Your mom had nothing to do with it."

"She stood there and watched you ruin my future," Kaylee spat out, her grief rising again and evident in her tone.

Mr. Dyer sighed again. "About eight years ago, your mom and I attended a gathering in Illinois. There we met Bay Weathers, the then chairman of the MLB. We talked with him for a long time, about you, your future. At the time we thought that it was our job to create your future. We didn't realize how dead wrong we were and that we were only destroying it for you. Well maybe not destroying it but making it a lot more difficult. We spoke about your passion and how you wanted to play in the major leagues. He encouraged your passion and wished you well, but we gave us a warning. He said that females tend to be exploited a lot in fields where there aren't many of them. The army, engineering, sports, there was just soo many stories. He told us a particular one of a lady who just like you, had wanted to be the first Major League Baseball player."

"What happened to her?"

"Good question. She died. And I'm not even making this stuff up, she hung herself in her bathroom. The pressure was just too much. Everyone who could give her an opportunity wanted something in return. These men, they don't go after regular ladies anymore. They want the high value women. It's like a game for them. On the drive back your mom wanted us to discuss it with you first but I had already made a decision.

That was why I canceled your application to that baseball college and tried to get you into Yale. I thought over there you'd be so occupied with school that all this just wouldn't matter anymore. When you told me you were going anyway I canceled your allowance because I thought it would make you stay. I forgot that you are a strong woman. And you can do anything you want."

By now, Kaylee was shedding more tears. She had never thought she'd live to see the moment when her parents would be truly sorry about all they did to her.

"I am so sorry Kaylee for everything I made you pass through. It was wrong of me as a father and it was just really a terrible thing to do. I don't know how I could ever make it up to you. But I promise I will try, I will do my very best. Please don't hold anything against your mother. She truly loves you and has cried and prayed for your return ever since you left. She misses you. I miss you. Could you ever find a place in your heart to forgive me?" Mr. Dyer said with teary eye.

Kaylee tried to wipe tears from her eyes but they were still flowing. Mr. Dyer didn't wait for a response, he simply went in and gave her a tight hug which she returned.

"I love you baby girl," Mr. Dyer said.

"I love you too dad," Kaylee mentioned.

"You know, I don't think I ruined your life. Look at you. You're a strong and beautiful woman who knows how to stand up for herself. You're a major league player and you did all of this by yourself."

"I'm a major league player who's about to be fired."

"Not if I can help it."

"What are you gonna do?"

"I've got a few tricks up my sleeve."

Kaylee smiled, she knew fully well that if her father said he would solve the problem, then he would solve it. He had proven himself many times in the past.

"How'd you even know I was missing?" Kaylee finally asked.

"Your journalist friend, he is very determined," Mr. Dyer replied. "He's a great guy Kaylee. He went through a lot to find you. Don't loose this one."

"Yeah whatever dad," Kaylee said as she chuckled.

"Come on, let's play some baseball," he said, as he stood to his feet with unexpected enthusiasm. "For old times' sake."

"I'm really not interested," Kaylee muttered, her gaze fixed on the ground.

"Come on, just one game," her father insisted, undeterred. "We don't need any equipment. Remember you used to play with whatever you could find?"

Reluctantly, Kaylee accepted the metal rod he offered her, feeling a pang of nostalgia as memories of their impromptu games flooded back. With a flick of his wrist, her father send a rock soaring into the air, and Kaylee swung the rod with all her might, connecting with it in a satisfying thud.

They continued like this, her father tossing rocks into the air and Kaylee swinging at them with renewed determination. As they laughed and joked, the weight of Kaylee's worries seemed to lift, if only for a moment.

Unbeknownst to them, Ed and Mrs. Dyer watched from a distance, their hearts heavy with concern for Kaylee. Despite their differences, they shared a common goal: to see her happy and fulfilled. As the night wore on, Kaylee's laughter echoed through the empty stadium.

Chapter 11
The Game

Kaylee and Ed stirred from their deep slumber as the morning light filtered through the curtains, casting a soft glow in the room. The tranquility was shattered by a loud knock at the door, causing them to jerk upright in bed.

Ed's instincts kicked in immediately, and he reached for the baseball bat they kept by the bedside. Kaylee followed closely behind as they approached the front door cautiously, their hearts pounding in anticipation.

With a firm grip on the bat, Ed pushed the door open, ready to confront whatever awaited them on the other side. Standing there, with an air of confidence, was Daryl, dressed in a turtle and trench coat.

"I can teach you how to use that thing," he said, nodding towards the bat in Ed's hand. Kaylee exchanged a surprised glance with Ed, unsure of what to make of Daryl unexpected visit.

"Do you need something Daryl?" Kaylee demanded already annoyed.

"No, you need me."

"Excuse me? Who the hell do you think you are?"

"The man that is about to save your life, that's who. Now can I come in or not?"

Kaylee did not want to let him in, but she knew that if Daryl showed up like this, by himself, then he probably had something she would need. She gestured for him to come in and he did confidently, taking a seat and spreading himself on the sofa.

"Nice place. I should buy it," Daryl remarked.

"You're not gonna sit at my boyfriend's house and waste my team you hear me. Now what is it you wanted to say," Kaylee demanded, her voice laced with anger.

Ed smiled at the mention of the word 'boyfriend' and stood over Daryl with the bat. Daryl stared at him with an angry look.

"That's not necessary men," Daryl mentioned.

"Start talking brother," Ed replied.

"Not even a drink first, that's how y'all treat visitors around here?"

"You banged at my door by 7am in the morning, Daryl that is a robbery not a visitor. Now state your business."

"Alright, he wants to kill you!," Daryl said and ended by mimicking himself dropping a mic.

"Who wants to kill me?"

"Who the fuck do you think?"

"Mr. Mock?"

"No, the fucking janitor at the Lakers NBA stadium, yes Mr. Mock. Did you forget the man already? It's only been a week for God's sake."

"Why would he try to kill me? What did I do to him?"

"What did you do to him? Are you kidding me? You ruined the man. You don't ruin a billionaire."

"I'm sorry, how do you happen to know all this?"

Suddenly, Daryl remains quiet. He begins to turn around nervously as he plays with his fingers. Kaylee and Ed notice the nervousness and this only raises their suspicions.

"Daryl, how do you know that Mr. Mock wants to kill me?"

Daryl stares at her and Ed, hoping that Ed wouldn't smash the bat into his head after his statement. "Because I'm the person he sent to do it. I'm the one who set your house on fire. But killing your friend, that wasn't me. That was his macho body guards and a resort attendant from New Mexico."

Kaylee pulls back, against the urge to smash his head into the ground and pound him to pieces. Her eyes got swelled up and teary, all she wanted to do was kill him.

"You almost killed me," Kaylee said amidst tears.

"I know, and I'm sorry. I don't hate you, I don't hate anybody. I'm a good guy, I'm a family guy. I just get really bitter sometimes and he just used it to his advantage. And I'm working on myself. I want to change. That's why I'm here to help you."

"You can start by telling us his next plan," Ed said as he circled back to the front of the sofa where Daryl was seated.

"I really don't know that. But I know that you should probably stay in here, lock your doors or something until you're safe. He doesn't want you to ever play a baseball game ever. And if he can't get your life, he'll try to destroy your body. Make sure you can't even move talk less play the game. He wants to frustrate you Kaylee, make you give up."

"I'm gonna meet him," Kaylee said sternly.

"Are you crazy?" Ed spat at her.

"I need to end this."

"You can't do that, you're a..."

"A woman, yeah? Isn't that what you were gonna say?"

"That's not what I meant. I don't want to see you hut."

"As much as I hate this, he's right. The team needs you. You're a good player. I still think you can do well in this league. It'd be sad to see you die. And Mr. Mock, will kill you for sure. Without even thinking about it."

"I'm counting on it," Kaylee said with an angry frown.

Kaylee's hand trembled slightly as she headed into the bedroom and reached for her jacket, her mind still reeling from the confrontation with Daryl. She barely spared a glance for Ed, who was clad only in his lower inner wear, before she pushed past them and made her way to the door. Daryl's attempt to stop her was met with a forceful shove, and Kaylee stormed out of the apartment without a backward glance. Inside the room, Ed rushed to grab a pair of pants, his movements quick and urgent as he processed the situation.

By the time Daryl emerged from the room, Kaylee was already in the elevator, the doors closing ominously behind her.

"Hold it, Kaylee. Hold it!" Daryl yelled at her. But Kaylee was stubborn and unwilling to be stopped. She had grown tired Mr. Mock's threats at her life as ready to square up with him, she didn't care about his status anymore or the control he had. She had forgotten that he did not even stay in Boston and of a truth, she had no idea about what she was trying to do.

With a sense of urgency, Daryl sprinted towards the stairwell, his heart pounding with each step he took.

As Kaylee stepped out of the building onto the sidewalk, her eyes scanned the area for a taxi. The street was eerily quiet, save for the distant sounds of traffic. Daryl emerged from the building just as she flagged down a passing cab, his breath coming in ragged gasps.

"Kaylee, wait!" he shouted at the top of his lungs, his voice strained with urgency. But Kaylee ignored him, her focus solely on escaping the turmoil of the moment and getting to Mr. Mock as fast as she could.

As the cab pulled away, Daryl's gaze swept across the street, his instincts on high alert. Something about the figure standing across from them seemed off as his hand went deep into his jacket. Without a moment's hesitation, Daryl rushed towards Kaylee, his heart pounding in his chest. Suddenly, the tranquility of the moment was shattered by the deafening sound of a gunshot.

Time seemed to slow as Daryl felt the impact of the bullet rip through his body, a searing pain flooding his sense. With a choked gasp, he stumbled forward, his vision blurring as darkness closed in around him.

Kaylee's scream echoed in his ears as he fell to the ground, his strength ebbing away with each passing moment. Through the haze of pain, he felt her presence beside him, her hands trembling as she reached out to him.

"See, I told you I'm a good guy," Daryl whispered hoarsely, his voice barely audible above the chaos. Kaylee's eyes filled with tears as she nodded, her heart breaking at the sight of him lying there, wounded and vulnerable.

"You are," she replied, her voice choked with emotion. "You are."

Meanwhile, Ed emerged from the building, his eyes widening in shock as he took in the scene before him. With trembling hands, he fumbled for his phone, his fingers moving frantically as he dialed 911. As the chaos unfolded around them, Kaylee remained by Daryl's side. And as the sirens wailed in the distance, signaling the arrival of help, Kaylee clung to the hope that somehow, they would make it through this ordeal together.

———◦———

AS KAYLEE STIRRED FROM her sleep, she found herself wrapped in Ed's comforting embrace. The warmth of his body against hers brought a fleeting sense of solace, but as she lay there in the darkness, her mind churned with turmoil.

Gently extricating herself from Ed's arms, Kaylee slid off the bed, careful not to disturb his slumber. She tiptoed across the room, her heart heavy with the weight of her thoughts.

Stepping into the living room, Kaylee was greeted by the soft glow of the moonlight streaming through the window. The city below sparkled like a sea of stars, casting a spellbinding aura over the landscape. Leaning against the windowsill, Kaylee gazed out at the city skyline, her mind adrift in a sea of memories. She recalled the countless nights she had spent, wrestling her dreams and aspirations, and the battles she had fought and was still fighting to chase them.

Baseball had always been her refuge, her sanctuary in times of uncertainty. From the moment she first picked up a bat, she knew she was destined for greatness. But now, faced with the harsh realities of life, Kaylee found herself questioning everything she had ever believed in. The recent events had taken their toll on her, leaving her feeling lost and adrift. She wondered if she had what it took to overcome the obstacles that lay ahead, or if she was destined to be swallowed by the tide of doubt and despair.

But deep down, Kaylee knew she couldn't give up- not now, not ever. She had worked too hard, fought too long, to let her dreams slip through her fingers. She refused to be a victim of circumstance, to succumb to the doubts and fears that threatened to consume her. It had been a week since the incidence with Daryl and he was getting better at the hospital. She had gotten news that Mr. Mock was in town, along with the MLB chairman for a meeting with the Boston Red Hawks management team. After all, he still owned the team, he just did not have any control over it.

With a determined resolve, Kaylee brewed herself a cup of coffee, the rich aroma filling the room with its comforting embrace. The familiar scent calmed her nerves, grounding her in the present moment.

After showering and dressing in a bold ensemble that reflected her adorning body, Kaylee left a note for Ed on the table- a simple message that spoke volumes: "I have to deal with this, no more hiding."

Setting an alarm for the next hour, Kaylee made her way out of the apartment, her steps firm and purposeful. She didn't know where she was going or what lay ahead, but she was determined to face whatever challenges awaited her head-on.

As she stepped out into the cool night air, Kaylee felt a surge of adrenaline coursing through her veins. The world seemed to shimmer with possibility, beckoning her to embrace the unknown with open arms. With each moment, Kaylee felt herself growing stronger, more resilient in the face of adversity. She knew that the road ahead would be fraught with challenges, but she also knew that she had the strength and courage to overcome. A taxi parked in front of the building and whisked her away.

————◉————

AS KAYLEE STEPPED OUT of the taxi and onto the grand driveway leading up to Elton Mock's prestigious rented mansion, she couldn't help but feel a mix of apprehension and determination. She always wondered why he never stayed in hotels but always rented out large mansions for small time stays. It was probably part of his schemes to gain privacy while he abused women. She however straightened her shoulders, smoothed down her outfit, and walked up to the imposing entrance.

The two towering bodyguards stood sentry at the door, their imposing presence making Kaylee feel small in comparison. They eyed her warily as she approached, but without a word, they stepped aside to allow her entry.

The moment Kaylee stepped into the opulent living room, she was struck once again by grandeur. Expensive furnishings adorned the space, and the walls were adorned with priceless artworks. Everything exuded wealth and luxury, a stark contrast to Kaylee's humble upbringing. She wished that all of his wealth would burn so Mr. Mock would stop tormenting people. As stepped in, she took off her jacket and flung it on the sofa, revealing her adoring curves behind a short and tight fitting outfit.

In the center of the room, Elton Mock stood, his imposing figure commanding attention. Despite the animosity between

178

them, Mr. Mock couldn't deny the magnetic pull he felt towards her. He turned to face her, his expression unreadable.

"Kaylee," he greeted, his voice smooth and velvety. "I must say, you're looking as enchanting as ever."

Kaylee fought to keep her composure as she met his gaze. Despite his welcoming demeanor, she couldn't shake the feeling of unease that settled in the pit of her stomach.

"Thanks for letting come on such short notice," Kaylee said with a seductive but deceptive smile.

Elton Mock's lips curved into a sly smile as he gestured for Kaylee to take a seat opposite him. She hesitated for a moment before complying, her senses on high alert. As they settled into their seats, Kaylee couldn't help but feel a sense of unease wash over her. She knew that beneath Elton Mock's charming facade lay a dangerous man, capable of manipulation and deceit.

"Quite a stare you've been causing these days," Kaylee said.

"Well, I had to get your attention somehow," Mr. Mock replied.

"You need my attention that bad?" Kaylee said as she rubbed his chest.

"You're a beautiful lady my dear, everyone needs your attention that bad."

"So bad that you're willing to take my life for it."

"Well when you put it like that. Look, it was never an attempt on your life. Just a few things to show you what a rich and powerful man can do."

"I see, well, you definitely got my attention. Now what are you gonna do with it?"

"You would never believe, my dear."

"Tell me, tell me all the things you want to do to me."

179

Mr. Mock hesitated, then took off his suit top and leaned closer. "I want to have you all to myself. I want to take you into my bedroom, I want to take off your clothes and throw them all across my room. I want to make love to you so much you'd loose your breath. I want all of you."

Kaylee stared at him seductively, making him truly believe that she wanted him too.

"Well what are you waiting for?" Kaylee asked.

Mr. Mock smiled, then tried to lean in for a kiss but Kaylee pressed her finger on his lips. "No, no, no, shirt off first," Kaylee said as she ran her fingers down his chest and lower down to his belly. Mr. Mock quickly took off his shirt without hesitation.

Kaylee then pushes him down until his laying flat on his back on the sofa, then she climbs on top of him. "Tell me again, what do you wanna do to me?" Kaylee said again, this time putting more effort into the seductiveness of her voice as she kissed his neck.

Mr. Mock glared at her with a smile, he was enjoying the moment. "I Elton Mock, wants to make love to you Kaylee Dyer."

'That was rather direct. That was weird right?' she thought to herself.

Suddenly, without any warning, Mr. Mock flung her to the side, landing her on the ground with a thud. He immediately got up and picked her jacket up then pulled out her phone and just as he suspected. It was recording. He immediately, deleted the recording and smashed the phone on the ground.

"NO!" Kaylee shouted out loud.

"You think you're a smart one," Mr. Mock remarked. "Oh you foolish foolish girl. You can't play me. I'm the fucking boss here. I don't need you. I can get any woman I want."

Mr. Mock suddenly landed her a hard slap on the face, followed by a punch. He pounced on her and began to beat her while she fought for her life.

"You don't ruin me and get away with it, you dumb brat," Mr. Mock said as he threw her against the sofa and slapped her again. Kaylee managed to push herself up and jump on him. She gave him a hard bite on his arm that made him yell out, but a hard pull on her hair did the trick and she was down on the floor again with another slap to the face.

Kaylee then took a vase and smashed it on his face, causing a cut on his cheek, but he was a hard man. He grabbed her and punched her on the belly. Then raised her again and pinned her to the wall, trying hard to choke her to death but Kaylee fought back, scratching at him with her finger nails. Then he gave her a hard punch to the face and grabbed a dagger from the stool which he threw at her, going straight for her chest but Kaylee grabbed his hand. They began to struggle as Mr. Mock pushed with all his might to get the dagger into her chest and Kaylee gave it everything she got to keep the dagger out.

"You are nothing Kaylee. You're not special, you're not skilled, you're not even a good player. You're gonna die like the others, with nothing," Mr. Mock yelled in his struggle.

A surprise suddenly spread on Mr. Mock's face the moment he saw her smiling.

"Oh death is funny to you huh?" he added.

"Maybe you're right. I don't have the things you have and maybe I never will. But I have friends, friends who are always there when I need them the most," Kaylee said as he smile finalized.

WHAM! A bat suddenly took Mr. Mock to the ground. He suddenly turned around to see Ed, Mel, Little John and Mark standing over him, all holding baseball bats.

"You ever got beaten by four six foot men before? It is not fun," Mel said with a grin.

Kaylee smiled as Mr. Mock's countenance changed to scared frown.

———◦———

AS THE EARLY MORNING light cast a soft glow over the front yard of Elton Mock's rented mansion, the scene was a flurry of activity. An ambulance was parked nearby, its doors open as paramedics tended to Kaylee's wounds at the back. Ed, Little John, Mark, and Mel stood around her, their faces etched with concern.

Kaylee winced as the paramedics applied antiseptic to her injuries, the pain sharp and searing. But she remained stoic, deciding to to push through the discomfort.

"You really shouldn't have left like that though," Ed mentioned.

"And miss my shot at getting the proof I needed, hell no," Kaylee replied.

"For real though, he could have killed you," Mel added.

"That's why I left him that alarm. I didn't expect him to call the whole neighborhood tho," Kaylee said. They all chuckled at this.

"Guess in the end, we didn't even need tax fraud and money laundering charges. Attempted murder works for me. Thank God for the law," Ed added with a grin.

They all laughed at this, enjoy the joys of the moment.

Meanwhile, multiple police cars were parked outside the mansion, their lights flashing in the dim light of dawn. Officers moved swiftly, securing the area and taking control of the situation.

At the center of it all, Elton Mock was being dragged out of the mansion by two stern-faced officers. His face and body looked beaten to a pulp. His once-arrogant demeanor had been replaced by a look of defeat, his eyes downcast as he was escorted away.

The two macho bodyguards, who had once stood as formidable sentinels at the entrance of the house, were now bound and tied up with heavy cords. The police struggled to loosen the knots, their efforts hampered by the thickness of the cords.

Despite the chaos, there was a sense of relief in the air. The ordeal was finally over, and justice was being served. Kaylee's assailant had been apprehended, and she was now receiving the medical attention she desperately needed. As the paramedics finished her wounds, Kaylee let out a sigh of relief. She looked up at Ed, gratitude shinning in her eyes. Without his quick thinking and bravery, the outcome could have been much worse.

Ed returned her gaze with a reassuring smile, his hand gently squeezing hers in silent support. Little John, Mark and Mel stood nearby, their expressions a mix of relief and exhaustion. With the situation under control, the police began to wrap up their investigation, taking statements from those involved and collecting evidence from the scene. As the first rays of sunlight broke through the clouds, a sense of calm descended over the front yard. For Kaylee and her friends, the ordeal was finally dealt with. They could breathe a sigh of relief knowing that justice had been served and that they could finally move forward from the traumatic events of the past few hours. She hoped that due justice would be served to Mr. Mock for all he had ever done to her and those she probably never heard off. If all went well, he would be facing death charges or a very long time in prison. Even though a lot of his money and assets would still be waiting for him when he got out, that was a time she was going to enjoy without thinking of the past or the future. Whatever would come next, she and her friends would be ready for it.

"Big game in three weeks, you gon be ready right?" Little John reminded.

"Oh no, not in this body. Besides, coach said I'm too broken to be playing games right now," Kaylee replied him.

The boys, except for Ed laughed at this.

"We got a little something that can help with that.

———◉———

KAYLEE STOOD AT THE entrance of the old stadium, her eyes wide with wonder as she took in the scene before her. The stadium, weathered by time and neglect, stood as a testament to the history of baseball. She could see the large men inside, some lifting weights, others practicing their swings, all of them exuding an air of determination and skill.

Beside her, Mel and Little John grinned, clearly pleased with Kaylee's reaction.

"What better way to learn the game than to start from the history?" Mel said, his voice filled with enthusiasm.

"Yeah, this is were a lot of us at the Red Hawks started. This place is home. This, is the birth place of Boston baseball," Little John added, feeling the air in the stadium.

Kaylee nodded eagerly, her excitement palpable. She had always been a student of the game, eager to soak up every bit of knowledge she could, and being in this historic stadium felt like a dream come true.

As they entered the stadium, Kaylee took in the sights and sounds around her. The sound of bats hitting balls, the thud of weights being lifted, the shouts of encouragement from the men as they pushed themselves to their limits – it all filled her with a sense of anticipation.

A few of the men walked up to Mel and Little John.

"Yo, yo, yo, look with the rich and famous dragged in," the oldest of the crew said as he exchanged fist bumps and pleasantries with the two.

"Hey, Chiko, how you been men?" Mel inquired.

"I've been good, Mel," the man answered, not bothering at all about Kaylee. "What brings you around these parts again young man?"

"Yo, this is Kaylee Dyer, she's one of us but we need to put her back on the levels..."

"You sure she's good to go, I hear fires can be pretty bad."

Kaylee wondered for a second how he knew that she was in a fire, but remembered again that the presence of the press was one of the earliest felt.

"No, she ain't good bro, that why we're here. I need you to fix her up. Get her bones together, getting healing and back on her feet again in two weeks."

The old man nods to show he understands the tax at hand. "Alright, we start today. Come, come on. We start right now."

The days that followed blurred together, each one filled with grueling workouts and intense training sessions. Kaylee threw herself into the regimen with everything she had, determined to prove herself worthy of the game she loved so much.

Mornings turned into evenings, and days into nights, but Kaylee's determination never wavered. She ran up steep hills, feeling the burn in her muscles with each step. She lifted heavy weights, pushing herself to new limits with each repetition. She stretched and twisted her body, testing its flexibility and strength.

In the afternoons, she would swim laps in the stadium's pool, feeling the cool water soothe her tired muscles. And in the evenings, she would practice hitting with the baseball against fast throwers, her eyes trained on the ball as it hurtled towards her.

At first, it was hard. Kaylee struggled with the intensity of the workouts, her body rebelling against the demands placed upon it. She grew tired easily, her focus wavering as exhaustion set in. She even began to frustrate the men who were supervising her, their patience wearing thin as she stumbled through the exercises.

There were moments when she wanted to give up, to admit defeat and walk away. But then, Ed would come over to her, his voice filled with encouragement and belief. He reminded her of everything she had overcome, of the strength and determination that had brought her this far.

With his words ringing in her ears, Kaylee would pick herself up and start again. This time, her focus was sharper, her determination unwavering. She refused to let tiredness or frustration hold her back, pushing herself harder and harder with each passing day.

And slowly but surely, she began to improve. Her hits grew stronger, her throws more accurate. She moved with a grace and fluidity that she had never known before, her body responding to the demands placed upon it with ease.

Finally, one evening as the sun dipped below the horizon, Kaylee stood at the pitcher's mound, a baseball in her hand. With a deep breath, she wound up and threw the ball with all her might, watching it as it sailed through the air and landed squarely in the hole.

A cheer went up from the men around her, their faces alight with pride and admiration. And as Kaylee turned to give Ed a high five, she knew that she had finally found her place in the game she love so much. This was just the beginning of her journey, the game was on Monday, two days from now and she knew she was fully prepared. She knew that was no limit to what she could achieve.

———◦———

THE MONDAY MORNING game was a highly anticipated event, drawing fans from far and wide to the prestigious home stadium of the Red Hawks. As the sun rose, the stadium slowly came to life, buzzing with excitement and anticipation. The stadium, with it capacity for 80,000 fans, stood tall and proud, its grandeur evident from miles away. The seats filled up quickly, the sea of red and blue jerseys blending together as fans poured in, eager to witness the showdown between the Red Hawks and the Philadelphia Bulls. Even Ed Oakley was pat of the large fan base at the seats, not as a reporter today but as a regular fan and Daryl was crocheting right beside him.

In the locker room, the Red Hawks prepared for battle. The team manager delivered a rousing pep talk, emphasizing the importance of teamwork, determination, and giving it their all on the field. The players listened intently, their eyes reflecting the fire burning within them as they geared up for the game ahead.

"...and most especially, make sure to have fun out there," the team manager concluded.

Emerging from the locker room, the Red Hawks were met with a deafening roar from the crowd. The fans rose to their feet, their cheers echoing throughout the stadium as they showed their unwavering support for their beloved team. The players soaked in the atmosphere, feeling the adrenaline coursing through their veins as they made their way onto the field.

Before the game began, there were per-game presentations to honor the teams and the sport of baseball itself. A stirring rendition of the national anthem filled the air, bringing a sense of unity and patriotism to the crowd. The announcer introduced each player, their names reverberating through the stadium as they took their positions on the field.

As the umpire took his position behind home plate, the tension in the air was palpable. The crowd fell silent, hanging on the edge of their seats in anticipation of the first play.

The Red Hawks took to the field with determination, their eyes locked on the prize as they prepared to face off against their opponents, the Philadelphia Bulls. The crowd erupted into cheers, their voices mingling with the sounds of the game as the players showcased their skills and athleticism. It would eventually come down to Kaylee Dyer and if she would be able to deliver a star performance at the game today and this thought drained her.

Breath in, breath out. Kaylee did her best to stay calm, as this was it, this was finally it. Even though she missed the entirety of spring training due to her little incident, Kaylee found she was not nerved at all about what she was about to do. She was going to finally play her first actual MLB game, against New York of all places.

Breath in, Breath out. This was everything she had ever dreamed. This was everything she trained for, looked forward to. She was a professional baseball, player, and was going to show the world who Kaylee Dyer really is. Breath in, Breath Out. No more waiting, the time was now. This was it, her first real taste of baseball. It has all come full circle from when she was five, to twenty eight.

Breath in, breath out. The bright lights of the stadium, especially compared to the dim locker room she was in, was almost blinding. Kaylee had to blink a few times to get used to them, her eyes still adjusting. She quickly got this under control and stood in a lien with her team as they waited for the posing team to show up and do the same. This was a game after all, not some sort of life-or-death situation,

Breath in, breath out. No more waiting, no more distractions. This was it. The other team had arrived and had lined up, and they were now singing the national anthem. They were almost there, Kaylee was on edge, waiting for the words she oh so anticipated. Then, they came. They were easy enough to miss, and many would look over them, but not Kaylee. Never.

"Play ball."

For those who had been paying attention, their roaring increased exponentially, causing those who hadn't noticed to roar in excitement as well. As this was. As a home game, they would be in the field first, and soon broke rank to take their positions. Kaylee made her way to the pitchers mount and took her place. She had no delusions she could repeat her feet from a few weeks ago, but it sure would be nice if she could.

As the first batter walked up to the plate, Kaylee took a moment to steady herself. He was a medium-sized black man with a shaved head, sporting the number 17 on his jersey. With a deep breath, she prepared to throw her first pitch of the game, a fastball overhand. The ball flew towards the plate with precision, catching the inside corner for a strike.

"Strike one," the umpire called out.

The crowd cheered on Kaylee's first strike of the day, it was turning out well after all. A smile crept on Kaylee's face as she retrieved the ball from the catcher. She had started strong, and she intended to keep it that way. For her next pitch, she opted for a curve ball, hoping to throw off the batter's timing. It worked like a charm, as the pitch dipped sharply into the strike zone, earning her a second strike.

"Strike two," the umpire yelled out again.

Feeling confident, Kaylee decided to mix things up with her third pitch, another fastball. But this time, it sailed a bit too close to the batter, who wisely chose to let it pass. The umpire call it a ball, much to Kaylee's frustration. She shook it off and refocused, determined to regain control of the count.

With the count now 2-1, Kaylee knew she had to make her next pitch count. She decided to unleash her slurve, a combination of a slider and curve ball, aiming for the outside corner of the plate. But once again, the pitch missed its mark, resulting in another ball.

"Damn," Kaylee muttered to herself, feeling the pressure mounting. She took a moment to compose herself, closing her eyes and taking a deep breath. As she opened her eyes, she knew she had to deliver a strike on the next pitch.

With renowned strength, Kaylee wound up and released the ball with all her might. It flew towards the plate, seeming to hang in the air for an eternity. The batter hesitated, unsure whether to swing, but it was too late. The umpire's call rang out through the stadium, declaring the batter out on strikes.

"Strike three, you're out!"

The Bulls fans fell into stunned silence, while the crowd of the Red Hawks supporters erupted into cheers and applause. Kaylee's teammates rushed to congratulate her as she made her way back to the dugout, her confidence soaring.

Meanwhile, in the stands, the atmosphere was electric. The sea of red and blue jerseys waved flags and banners, chanting Kaylee's name in unison. The excitement was palpable as the Red Hawks too an early lead in the game.

Back in the dugout, Kaylee's coach offered her a congratulatory fist bump. "Great job, Kaylee," he said with a grin. "Keep pitching like that, and we'll be unstoppable."

Kaylee nodded, her focus already shifting to the next inning. She had made a statement with her performance on the mound, and she was going to continue dominating the game. With her teammates rallying behind her, she knew they had what it took to come out on top.

As the game progressed, Kaylee settled into a rhythm on the mound, mixing up her pitches with precision and control. Each time she stepped onto the mound, she exuded confidence, inspiring her teammates to elevate their game.

In the stands, the atmosphere was electric, with fans on the edge of their seats with every pitch. The roar of the crowd echoed throughout the stadium, urging the Red Hawks to victory. But it was far from over, there was still a long way the Red Hawks had to go to win this game and their opponents weren't going to sit back and just let them take it.

It was now Kaylee's turn to hold the bat, everything had come down to this moment. She stood at home plate, her heart racing with anticipation as she faced off against the first opposing pitcher. He was huge and built with a body that looked like it was made of bricks. The stadium buzzed with energy, the roar of the crowd echoing in her ears as she gripped the bat tightly in her hands. This was her moment, her chance to prove herself on the biggest stage, but there was so much fear and pressure from already starting to win.

As the first pitch came hurtling towards her, Kaylee's eyes locked onto the ball with laser focus. She swung with all her might, but the pitch sailed past her, leaving her feeling frustrated and determined to do better on the next one.

With each pitch that followed, Kaylee's resolve only grew stronger. She focused on her breathing, drawing in deep breaths to calm her nerves and steady her hands. She knew that she had the skill and the talent to succeed, she just needed to stay focused and trust in herself.

As the pitcher wound up for another delivery, Kaylee felt a surge of adrenaline course through her veins. The Red Hawks fans all suddenly and unanimously stood up and begin yelling out her name. This brought tears to Kaylee's eyes, she was shoke by the respect and love that the Red Hawks crowd was showing her.

"You got this," Mel called out. "They believe in you."

She looked to the stands, swerving her eyes around until she found Ed and Daryl waving directly at her. Kaylee was suddenly filled with more energy. Memories of the past month flashed through her eyes, the drama with Mr. Mock and the team, meeting Ed, the death of her best friend, the attacks on her life, everything led up to a powerful surge of energy and vibe in her. She was going to do this, especially since everyone had proven to her that they believed in her, and not because of her looks. This was her moment to shine, and she wasn't about to let it slip away. With a powerful swing, she connected with the ball, sending it soaring into the outfield.

The crowd erupted into cheers as the ball sailed over the fence, a towering home run that brought the entire stadium to its feet. Kaylee couldn't help but smile as she rounded the bases, the cheers of the crowd echoing in her eyes. But her joy was short-lived as she saw the worried expressions on the faces of her teammates. They knew that this game was far from over, and they needed to stay focused if they wanted to come out on top.

As Kaylee returned to the dugout, she could feel the weight of the moment bearing down on her. This was her chance to prove herself, to show everyone what she was made of. She couldn't afford to let her nerves get the best of her now.

With each passing inning, the tension in the stadium grew palpable. The game was neck and neck, with both teams fighting tooth and nail for every run. Kaylee knew that she needed to stay focused if she wanted to help her team secure the win.

As final innings approached, Kaylee could feel the pressure mounting. This was it, the moment she had been training for her entire life. She took a deep breath and steadied herself, her eyes locked on the pitcher as he wound up for the final pitch.

The pitcher steadied himself. She studied his stance, he knew what he was doing, she could see that it was going to be a trick throw but wasn't sure how he would throw it. However, she wasn't going to take her eyes of the ball. WHOOP... the ball left the pitcher's hand with a slicing force through the air and headed straight at Kaylee. She watched carefully for a split second and studied the direction in slow motion. With all the strength she could muster, Kaylee swung the bat with everything she had. WHAM... the crack of the bat echoed through the stadium as the ball sailed through the air, heading straight for the outfield.

The crowd held its breath as they watched the ball soar, willing it to clear the fence and secure the victory for the Red Hawks. And then, with a resounding thud, it landed in the stands, caught by the careful hands of cute blonde with a shirt that had Kaylee's face on it, sending the crowd into a frenzy of cheers and applause.

KAYLEE'S GRAND-SLAM

As Kaylee rounded the bases, a sense of euphoria washed over her. This was it, the moment she had been waiting for. She had come through when her team needed her most, proving once and for all that she was a force to be reckoned with on the field.

As she crossed home plate, Kaylee as met with hugs and high-fives from her teammates, their smiles reflecting her own sense of accomplishment. They had done it, they have won the game, and Kaylee couldn't have been prouder to be a part of such an incredible team.

Kaylee's smiled stretched from ear to ear as she walked off the field, her heart still racing with the thrill of victory. She had just achieved a milestone in her professional baseball career, striking out her first player in a league game, and it was a moment she would cherish forever. The memory of the bater's stunned expression, the roar of the crowd, and the overwhelming sense of joy that filled her heart would stay with her for the rest of her life.

As the game continued, Kaylee's elation only grew. She would later learn that she had been the winning pitcher in a hard-fought 11-8 victory, a feat that earned her a standing ovation from both the fans and her fellow players alike, including Daryl. It was a moment of triumph that she would never forget, a validation of all the hard work and dedication she had poured into her craft.

After the game, as the players made their way back to the locker room, Kaylee was stopped by Little John, one of her teammates. His eyes were filled with admiration as he congratulated her on her performance.

"Hey Kaylee, you were amazing out there," he said, clapping her on the back. "I can't thank you enough for what you did for the team today."

Kaylee smiled modestly, feeling a warm glow of pride at his words. "Oh, it was nothing," she replied. "I just did my job."

But another teammate chimed in, echoing Little John's sentiments. "No way, Kaylee," he said, grinning. "You were a rock out there. We couldn't have won without you."

Kaylee's smile widened at the praise, feeling a surge of gratitude towards her teammates. It meant the world to her to know that she had their support and respect, especially as she navigated her way through her rookie season. She turned to look at Daryl but he wan't interested in the cheer, he only focused on taking off his jersey at his locker. Kaylee continued to stare at him until he turned around and noticed her, he gave her a nod and turned back to his business and that was all she needed.

Little John smiled back at her, his eyes twinkling with pride. "You're a natural, kid," he said, giving her a playful punch on the arm. "I have a feeling you're going to be a star in this league."

Kaylee simply smiled. "No problem, though I must say I am surprised. After all, you guys could have lost because of me."

Little John smiled, and a couple other teammates laughed.

"Not in a million years kid, not in a million years. You're right where you need to be, and you're gonna win us all the bloody games, and tournaments and awards there are in the whole goddamn MLB." The rest yelled their agreement aloud at Little John's statement.

The words filled Kaylee with confidence. She had always dreamed of making it big in professional baseball ever since her grandfather took her to her first MLB game, and now, with her first taste of success under her belt, she was more determined than ever to chase after her dreams.

The End

Don't miss out!

Visit the website below and you can sign up to receive emails whenever Joey Dolton publishes a new book. There's no charge and no obligation.

https://books2read.com/r/B-A-RDVBB-XXWBD

BOOKS 2 READ

Connecting independent readers to independent writers.

Also by Joey Dolton

About the Author

Joey Dolton is a captivating wordsmith with a penchant for exploring the uncharted realms of emotions and fear, and is a versatile author who seamlessly weaves the threads of romance, science fiction, and horror into a tapestry of gripping narratives. Born with a vivid imagination and an insatiable curiosity, Joey's literary journey has been marked by a fearless exploration of the human experience within the extraordinary

Publishing, LLC

About the Publisher

Boro Publishing, LLC is a small independent publisher, seeking to tell stories, both real and fictional. We want to tell everyone's story, and do it in the best way possible.